The Failure Myth: Success Unwritten

THE FAILURE MYTH: SUCCESS UNWRITTEN

Faux-Failure: A journey through fear, growth and self discovery

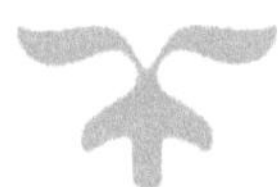

Contents

DEDICATIONS

*To those who stumble through the labyrinth of life,
who falter, question, and seek clarity in the midst of chaos,
only to face greater odds but continue their pursuit.*

To those who fail while striving, yet keep trying.

The Faux-Failure Playlist

1. Stand By You by Rachel Platten
2. Fight Song by Rachel Platten
3. Stronger by Kelly Clarkson
4. Like A Champion by Selena Gomez
5. Rise by Katy Perry
6. Rise Up by Andra Ray
7. Rise by Selena Gomez
8. Firework by Katy Perry
9. Brave by Sara Bareilles
10. Believer by Imagine Dragons
11. Mirrorball by Taylor Swift
12. My Mind and Me by Selena Gomez
13. You're on your own kid by Taylor Swift
14. Look what you made me do by Taylor Swift
15. ...Ready for it? by Taylor Swift
16. On My Way – Alan Walker, Farruto, Sabrina Carpenter
17. DON'T YOU WORRY by Black Eyed Peas , Shakira
18. So Am I by Ava Max
19. Love Myself by Hailee Steinfield
20. **This is me Trying by Taylor Swift**

INTRODUCTION

About two years ago, I started writing to explore what it feels like to be in the head of a teenager navigating the tumultuous journey into adulthood. Through conversations with countless individuals who found themselves in similar situations, I envisioned a character named Ahmad, living in the small city of Srinagar, India. The responsibility of telling this story raw left me with few choices to fictionalize, and I believe I did what I could.

The journey in **Faux-Failure** picks up right where my previous work ended, delving into a specific and intense topic: the Joint Entrance Examination (JEE), an exam that weighs heavily on the minds of countless students in India. This book captures the essence of a young man grappling with a life that appears less fortunate due to past experiences, struggling against the will to take a test that "might decide his fate."

What lies ahead for Ahmad isn't just a test of knowledge; it becomes a trial of endurance, resilience, and survival in a world where success feels like the only option. Every day, Ahmad spirals into the 'what ifs'—what if he isn't good enough? What if failure is his only outcome? The weight of expectations, both his own and those of the world around him, forms a heavy fog that clouds his every step. It's not just the JEE exam that looms ominously over him; it's the profound fear of never being enough, of falling short and losing himself in the chaos of his mind. This journey isn't merely about passing or failing—it's about holding on to his identity in a system that allows little room for mistakes.

There's no public agenda in this narrative; my aim is to present a vivid portrayal of Ahmad's life as he navigates the intricate world of the JEE. I've once again had the privilege to be in a similar situation and connect with people from diverse backgrounds, each story contributing to the single mixture of experiences surrounding the JEE.

While reading this book, I invite you to recognize the personal opinions interwoven throughout. If you can distinguish these perspectives, it may resonate with your own beliefs and experiences.

Regardless of the primary focus, the overarching message of **Faux-Failure** seeks to understand how to gracefully live with failure and find a way to progress. When we fall short, the feeling of failure can be overwhelmingly real. **Faux-Failure** embodies the concept of feeling like you've failed in the moment, yet realizing in hindsight that it was not a failure at all. Instead, it may have helped you uncover and achieve a higher purpose in life. Most people online suggest that whatever happens, happens for a reason, and it's acceptable to fail; you simply need to dust yourself off and keep moving forward. However, the essence of this narrative lies in recognizing that you don't have to deny your feelings of failure or run away from them. It's about validating your emotions, acknowledging the pain of falling short, and still pushing through despite feeling torn apart.

Faux-Failure gives you the liberty to experience all those emotions without cringing at your retrospection. Failure feels real, and while it may seem insurmountable, acknowledging your struggles while powering through them is an integral part of the journey.

Artistic imagination of Faux-Failure

The reality keeps shooting back

And the despair of what could've been wrecks.

The hope is cruel. It cracks open the half healed wounds and shoves a bunch of rusty salt inside them.

It reminds you of what could've been if something would've been.

But every time you wake up from the dream and do all you can to keep going with your day, even if that means giving it up.

It's like time travel, the hope.

It's the smell and sound of sizzling hot and delicious food

It's the far view mirage to a person quenched with thirst in a dessert.

It's the sound of people coming from far away to a person stranded in a forest.

The time period in which you make up the fantasy that perhaps you get what you hope for is stretched into hours, only to realise at the end that fate budges

And you end up accounting no memory to the breaths that you took during the whole time.

THE BURDEN OF EXPECTATIONS

Chapter One

Time, like the finest grains of sand, slips through our fingers with an elusive swiftness, never to return once gone. Its value lies not in its mere passing but in the opportunities and experiences it presents. Each passing second is a precious fragment of existence—a chance to learn, to love, and to grow. As the minutes cascade into hours and days, they remind us of the fleeting nature of our journey. To grasp the significance of time is to appreciate its finite nature and strive to make every tick of the clock count. Yet, despite this understanding, we often fail to execute this wisdom in our lives, leading to circumstances we may regret.

My 12th-grade exams had just concluded, and it was time for a much-needed and well-earned break. I intended for it to be short since JEE preparation was on the horizon.

However, that was not the case. During a conversation with Gagan, she remarked, "I don't think coaching institutes will start the enrollment process anytime soon." Trusting her judgment, I slowed down my plans. The break soon became monotonous, and I wasted time mindlessly scrolling the internet—completely opposite to what I had envisioned.

One day, I decided to pick up *The Alchemist*, a book I had planned to read post-exams. It was a moving tale, and one idea that struck me was how sometimes we must undertake unplanned or unpleasant tasks to achieve our ultimate goals. I tried to internalize this concept, seeing the JEE test as a step toward my dream of pursuing research. Yet, reading the book did little to curb my time-wasting habits.

I had applied for online scholarship submissions for JEE coaching, a process that seemed interminable. Then, I learned that *The Hikers Coaching Institute*, known in Kashmir for JEE preparation, had started its enrollment process. Panic struck me—my default response to anything new. I quickly got the institute's contact number via Instagram and called. A lady confirmed that admissions were still open. However, upon reading reviews online, I discovered a screening test was required—a numerical paper that sent me spiraling. My exams had been over for a month, and I felt unprepared. In desperation, I texted Heidi, venting, "How on earth do I study everything overnight and pass this test?"

Discussing my future plans with my family always felt awkward; they seemed overly protective, shielding me in a bubble at the expense of my growth. Yet, I mustered the courage to tell my dad about the situation. His initial response was, "But the results aren't even out yet. What's the point?" Reluctantly, I explained the urgency and convinced him.

The next day, I dressed and headed to Hikers. On the way, my mind buzzed with concerns about the distance. I reassured myself that it was similar to my high school commute, but the sunny day and my layered clothing made me feel like wilted spinach. At the institute, I registered for the screening test. However, there was a catch: "We can't enroll you based on the screening test alone. You'll need to pay the admission fees upfront or wait for the scholarship results, but sessions won't wait for scholarship students." Their words, laced with passive aggression, left me at a crossroads.

The test itself was daunting. The numerical questions seemed alien, and chemistry—a subject I usually found manageable—felt nightmarish. The room's temperature didn't help either. I scraped together a meager 60 marks out of 360. Two days later, the institute called to inform me I'd passed, though in hindsight, I realized the screening was just a formality. Still, I decided to wait for the scholarship results.

The wait was excruciating. Friends would message me about their progress at Shining Star coaching, heightening my anxiety. The institute's calls, urging me to secure a seat, only added to the stress. Their promise of limited seats and "exclusive" classrooms of

60 students felt hollow, as my eventual batch had over 150 students.

During this time, I attempted self-study, but my perfectionism paralyzed me. I flitted between topics, overwhelmed by the syllabus. Exhausted and demotivated, I stopped altogether, convincing myself to take another break. I deactivated Instagram, decided to chill, and started photoshopping to distract myself.

One day, Gagan revealed she had the scholarship results PDF. Elation washed over me as if chains had been broken. I immediately informed my dad, and we visited the institute to finalize my enrollment. We also arranged for transportation, which taught me a valuable lesson: if you don't ask for what you want, you won't get it.

As the day ended, we stood waiting for a rickshaw, and the winter evening closed in. None showed up initially, but eventually, we found one. Back home, I updated Gagan about the experience. She disapproved of the institute's five-day-a-week schedule, a sentiment I would come to understand in hindsight.

Chapter Two

The drive came through, and there was a girl in the car, Sabrina, we didn't talk much at first but then at one point she asked, "Why are you so late to join the course?" I dodged the question saying that it wasn't much, without offering a valid explanation, and it was settled. We reached the institute; I was obliged to show up with a document in the office, so I asked one of the workers, "Where's the office?"

"This way," he pointed to the end of the hallway.

I entered the office to find no one in there, so I waited outside, pacing the corridor every once in a while to avoid the feeling I was getting as people would stare at me. I didn't know how to properly use the official website, and they hadn't updated their schedule on the notice board either that day, and I went down this rabbit hole that maybe I don't even have classes that day, 'how am I going to go back home' and all kind of thoughts I have when I go to a new place and meet new people kicked in. After spending what felt like forever in the corridor, a guy wearing glasses and a suit- probably the manager- came down the stairs and asked me what I was doing there, "I have to show my documents," I said to him and he suggested that I should go to the class and show my papers after the classes were over, so I headed towards my class which was on the fourth floor from the ground floor and fucking hell climbing those stairs was such an ordeal! I was wearing a jacket and a turtle neck, yes again, I never stopped wearing that combo, I was out of breath and drenched in sweat; two more people were heading to the same class, I walked behind them so that I wouldn't get noticed by all the people in the class, I entered the room, and this colossal heat wave hits my face and I walked the aisle of benches towards the back of the room because none of the front row seats were vacant. I had to sit on one of those back benches as I felt a wire short-circuit inside my head, and the classroom was huge with all these people and suffocation resembling the atmosphere of the inside of an oven. As I sat down drenched in sweat; after climbing the stairs, and panting of being completely out of breath, it took me one long minute to get hold of myself and even out the panting.

These two people who I came with started playing games on their mobile phones, and I was disturbed by the whole setting; the teacher was teaching 'Structure of an atom', and the class already had completed most of the chapter; The teacher was pretty cool though, and he ended up becoming a friend later in the course and my favorite teacher of the institute, Anirudh. One thing that I was carrying with me besides the baggage and self-sabotage that day was my poop. Yeah, that's right, I was sitting in the class, struggling to make notes while holding my poop. But I couldn't hold it any longer. Hence, I stood up and asked the teacher permission to go to the restroom, and the whole class stopped in that moment in time. Everybody was staring at me as if I had passed a death sentence, but the teacher, in a very relaxed manner replied by saying, "You do not have to ask for permission to go anywhere, not at least in my class," he immediately made out that I was 'the newest one in the class', now the new struggle was to find the restroom, I had to rush down the stairs and ask one of the worker. I don't know if it was because I was freaking out or because I was losing my mind because of the poop that I pointed towards the elevator for clarification, I knew it was the elevator, but I just wanted him to point me into the right direction, and he naturally laughed on me. A REAL STRUGGLE indeed.

Sharon bursts out laughing and says, "Well, I'm kind of liking this part of the story for all the humor, but how exactly do you remember it in such a hilarious way?"

"Well, it sure as hell didn't seem hilarious to me when it was happening, but because I had lowered my standards and expectations towards myself significantly that the insult didn't feel bad and was unquestionable to stress about. Besides I'd had had a blast in the year prior that definitely shifted the mind-set, it makes you calm, till the effect lasts."

Sharon and I have been talking since the morning and it's three in the afternoon. We got so invested that at one point, Sharon called the receptionist girl and asked her to clear the schedule for the rest of the day. She said she only meets people who have been coming into therapy for a long time today and that they could come next (this day next week too). Naturally, neither of us didn't even have our lunch. So here I am, in my car, waiting for the pizza that I ordered and I take out my phone to take a look at the google calendar because that keeps me sane. Although there are still some days that I get so caught up with the planning to the last detail that if sometimes some important thing pops up, I tend to lose it, but I have worked on it over the years, besides there's always Alisha to keep my feet on the ground and head in the right direction. She taught me how to live spontaneously while also at the same time being responsible and bearing the load of deadlines that require excessive planning. I think about last night and I write in my notes app that I am going to text her, and a notification pops up and it's the text from her.

"Hii. Guess you're not going to text me and tell me where you are?"

"Oh, hey, Hun. Wasn't expecting the text baby."

"Well, deal with it! What did you do? Are you done with the session? What did Mr. Sebastian tell you?"

"Woah! Slow down, angry bird. Sorry for snapping at you yesterday. I should have been a little more patient. And, uh, about Mr. Sebastian, he wasn't here, not in the morning at least."

"Babe... What? Where have you been all day? I locked the house, did you come back? Where are you then?"

"Don't worry, the question is where you are?"

"On my way to pick up the kids from Heidi's."

"Well don't, how about you come here, see we have a lil' situation, Mr. Sebastian wasn't here in the morning but there was this middle aged woman she was very nosey, so I had to evaluate all my choices and I landed on this other therapist...Btw, lemme say this, great therapist. The best one there is.

So yeah, I knew you'd get angry, so I ended up booking an appointment with her and you will never believe the milestones that we have hit so far. And she happens to know you,

very well. You need to come. And babe sorry, and I missed you, and I could really have you here."
"But what about kids?"
"Well pick them up when we're done here, or maybe they can stay the night at Heidi's."

*****

You see, I always hated a lot of stimulation that also used to encompass interactions with people who were…normal? They were happy, having fun, laughing, cracking jokes, but as long as you don't know how it feels like at the other end of the tunnel, its baseless to think of even crossing it, you think it is as good as it gets, and there's no point of doubting your reality, because you have nothing to base the contradiction on. I was sitting with a bunch of back-benchers who were literally playing games in the class; it was a lot to take in. We had a quick ten-minute refreshing break, and people I was sharing my bench with called upon their friends, and then it became a whole thing. I somehow gathered my shit together and asked one of the guy there about the completion of the syllabus; he told me that they had done an average of one and a half chapters in each subject; I tried not to panic or get anxious or any of those things so I just breathed onto it meanwhile the physics class started, the teacher was in a hurry, and he quickly jumped towards the board- something Jamshed Sir would never do, an immediate red flag- he had scheduled two back-to-back physics classes. He was teaching something in force and laws of motion which was bouncing the hell over my tiny little stupid head. He would glance at me every minute or so because of the seating arrangement I was in; it definitely comes with a reputation, and let's just say I don't like that; he might have thought that I was just any other back-bencher who had come there to create chaos while at the same time he might have been shocked by why was I putting up a show of being attentive and the same old pang of feeling alien-like settled in; the whole setting was chaotic.

I was struggling in real-time to take and make notes because of how fast he was going, and on top of that, he was midway through the chapter, which made it even more difficult. I got frustrated and couldn't even ask a question because I thought it wouldn't reach- for the room was enormously big- and that lecture shattered my confidence the same way a glass disintegrates into tiny little pieces when it falls to the floor, and even if you were to put the pieces together the bruises are still visible. Now the thing with me is that I do not just feel bad, I become miserable and depressed and not just for one thing in particular but the thing is that my thoughts get deluded and I'll get triggered from a memory from the past that made me feel the same way and I end up getting devastated, it's a feeling as if I'm walking down some sort of aisle and every single thing that I've done wrong is on the either side of the aisle and each one of my bad memories replays itself with each step I take, and that is what happened, I began to doubt my decisions of even being there in that exact moment, I thought how my admission was so late which had made me miss out on certain topics, I felt like turning and twisting in the seat while this replay in my head of how I hadn't learnt much in shining star started to play, I felt like I was in the wrong place and all of this further raised my already high temperature and I had no other choice but to take deep breaths and calm down to put a stop to this memory-slideshow if I wanted to not turn into a maniac. I remember he gave some practice questions and how I couldn't even figure out where I had to start from, forget about trying I was not even able to keep up with his pace, so much so that I couldn't even write the questions correctly; he would only draw the schematic figure and dictate the numeral details real fast. He looked in my direction and saw me struggling with the questions and said, "Only making notes won't do you any good; you've got to solve the questions also," followed by a bold statement, or a claim, he suggested, almost ordered that, "You have to only sleep for the duration of three to four hours a day and practice the questions in the remaining time," he supported the statement by adding, "none of you guys have practiced any numerical question in the span of last two years that's why you guys need this much practice every single day."

Now when a teacher makes a statement like that while also you have been an "A-lister," you are to take it seriously and act accordingly, but having said that I am a seven-hour-sleep guy, I need seven hours of daily sleep, no average, exact seven hours, to feel like a human being, at that point the memories of twelfth grade were still fresh which included me learning a lesson of not compensating the studies and sleeping less, so my head was clear, but again when a teacher tells you something, they're putting themselves out there while making a statement, it's a serious thing, and you treat it seriously, it forms its place in the back of your mind even if you don't realize. After the classes were over, I went to him to figure out a strategy to cope with the syllabus I had missed; he said the same thing the kid had said.

At this point, it's evident how worried I was for the syllabus completion, desperate even. I left the classroom, went to the office to show the document, and left the building. I texted Hiedi over Snapchat, and she asked about the day; I filled her in with the necessary details sparing the miserable ones and headed home.

The next day I took a front-row seat, and there was a guy wearing glasses and a cap that read DOPE; he was very gentle with the way he asked me for my name, and he would add something every once in a while during the lecture. The chemistry teacher, Mr. Anirudh, was onto the last part of the chapter; I had missed the rest of it, so noting down didn't feel significant; needless to say, I couldn't understand anything he was saying as if he was teaching some rocket science and like I had not just qualified twelfth grade with that subject.

Usually, it would not been this way; if I couldn't get what the teacher was saying, it's either I had a doubt or a misunderstanding, or the teacher had it wrong, but that was no longer the case; the teacher was absolutely accurate as people were asking him questions and he was replying to each one of them, and everybody's doubts were getting cleared, so evidently this time it was me who was to blame, it was not just a doubt or misunderstanding, It was a realization that I'm late, very late and it is hard to cope-up with the stuff now. As the class was over, the teacher left, and the guy sitting next to me, Suhaeeb, asked the other guy sitting right next to him to give him his notebook so he could catch up on the syllabus, which that guy denied! "I won't give you my notebook," I heard him saying. I was alarmed and thunderstruck to hear that a person wouldn't give their notebook because, for me personally, I have always been a guy who would share my notes with anyone. He was immediately a huge red flag, my head felt big and red like a magically inflated red balloon about to blow all the steam off, it was a sudden realization that self-centered people like him would surround me on this journey.

I spent the rest of the classes mourning inside my head for the circumstances and people my fate had landed me into. Physics felt totally strange to me, and so did maths. Although, I don't have much to say about math because I had known beforehand that I hadn't studied Jee-level mathematics and that it would be very difficult. I was mentally prepared for that, but physics and that teacher, Mr. Sarfaraz, would get on my nerves. As I was riding towards home, I was all dull and gloomy from the inside; I had started to loathe my decision to enroll there, I reached home and had my lunch, and soon after that, I went upstairs into my room, I remember feeling so down as if I had awakened one day to find out that everyone on the planet had gone, and I was the only one left- alone and stranded. I started having flashbacks on how me and my other friends at shining star would sit together and we would copy from one another's notebook if any one of us had had missed something, in fact anybody would come to us and clear their doubts but here I was I had joined a new coaching institute, a new world with new people and then I started crying, it was so spontaneous that I couldn't stop, there was only one thing that I could think of doing at that time, texting my old friends and telling them how lonely I feel.

"I feel abandoned here and there's no one whom I could call my friend" all while I was wiping my tears, I told them that I missed them and how it had been the biggest mistake of my life to leave shining star and join Hikers, but there was a little voice at the back of my head, probably my conscience to remind me that leaving Shining star was not a wrong decision after all because of how terrible and out of place the blonde-hair always made me feel but that didn't stop me from complaining, at Shining star I at least knew most people and I could talk to anybody anytime but here, things were south, the two scenarios were like the two faces of the coin ; I didn't know anybody there, couldn't get what teachers were saying most of the time, they would rather see me as a class-liability to direct their attention towards me, I couldn't ask my doubts, didn't have any friends and being surrounded by some self-centered people was a horrible nightmare.

"I didn't even try to not cry because what I had established the year before is that when I cry, I suddenly feel relaxed, and I no longer seem to experience any emotional pain that I had experienced moments before."

"Well, I guess you must know that there's some actual science behind it; it's not a made-up concept," Sharon says, and I nod because the therapist that I went to when I was nineteen told me about it. Honestly, I would have done it nonetheless because I knew there was just something about it that hit the right parts.

*****

The next day I took a seat in the middle because I wasn't feeling quite comfortable sitting at the edge of the bench, so I asked Suhaeeb to swap seats. He ever so gently did, or so I thought but little did I know that he had been distracted by that girl sitting at the other end of the aisle, all along and just wanted a better view of her; he would talk a lot during the classes and ask me a truck load of questions, and sitting in the front row seat, everybody would think that we were gossiping, sometimes his question asking would also mean that I would have to completely shift my attention towards him which would result in me getting distracted, but I could never say no to him; he was innocent and trusting, and I didn't want to break his heart; I thought it would be rude if I refused.

It was within the first week itself that, once again, a government official "notification regarding the closing of coaching institutes" was issued- although I had a different name for it, my doom. The main reason besides me being not interested in jee that I had ended up ignorant had been the online learning mode so the news wasn't exactly blissful; yet again my demons took over my mind that transitioning from Shining Stars to Hikers would go in vain, at least I had some familiar faces at Shining star, and I was well versed with the teaching style of every lecturer. My next thought was my brain screaming at me, "Ayo! You are not able to raise any doubts sitting in the physical classroom. How the hell will you be able to raise them in a virtual class?" But as it was the government decision, there was no choice; we spent the next hour installing the application that we were going to attend our zoom class on. The online classes were to resume within two days, but here's the critical part, the highlight of that day; while I was doing some questions in physics on my own, I had a couple of doubts, so I asked the guy. The same guy who refused the notes, and ironically, he was very supportive and helped me solve that problem. We talked to each other; we exchanged our Instagram handles, and it turned out to be a great experience overall. I remember feeling guilt from the inside because I had considered him a bad person.

"Well, now that I think of it, Suhaeeb told me that Sehran had refused to give his notebook."

"You see the tricks the brain plays? I would not call it a trick; it makes you think that you're in some danger and you try to do everything in your power to avoid the coming danger, and in this situation you convinced yourself that he was a bad person. But at the same time one also has to be conscious of these biases of the brains because our demons are also created by our brains, an example being procrastination, but we have to be able to see through it and do the right thing."

Chapter Three.

Initially, I thought the classes would be boring and unproductive online, but then I had a change of heart because it felt like I was Catastrophizing and needed to keep an open mind and stay optimistic. Chemistry was our first-ever online class; we started a new chapter, and as I already said we had the coolest teacher for chemistry; he had a bunch of tricks up his sleeves that gave us a headstart in chemistry, and everybody would join his class; he taught us ways to solve problems in simple ways and I personally got to learn quite many things as I was blank page when I got there, I didn't know about most of the parts that existed in the textbook, and I had qualified the grade. Physics went well on the first day; we had no math class for the next few days because the teacher was Covid-positive. What I had thought of as a catastrophe turned out to be a good thing because I started raising questions, and the teachers would answer them; Anirudh shared his telegram handle with us, saying, "Text me any time of the day, and I will try to clear your doubt," wasn't lying though. Within a day or two, chemistry started to feel like home; I would ask the doubts and answer the questions, but at the same time, physics started to get boring; the teacher got fast again, which was intimidating. Those beginning days were hopelessly undelightful and bizarre, everybody at home, one after one, caught cold; yeah, me too which resulted in me dreading attending those physics lectures, one day I got annoyed and I eventually stopped logging into physics lectures, but at the same time, I started watching the three-hour YouTube lectures in an attempt to clear my basics over attending Mr. Sarfaraz's lectures. I had made this ritual of making micro notes on weekends, which I would follow religiously, but I hadn't been one hundred percent productive all this time; I had started to be active on Instagram since the classes had shifted to online mode, I gave myself explanation that I didn't have any commute time, and as a result I would be distracted here and there; starting out it wasn't very significant to show in my day-to-day behaviour but it did affect me nevertheless. I got the material from the institute and started solving the starter exercise although the past archives and the accelerator would give me a hard time (that was why I had decided to watch online lectures in depth so that I could solve all the questions). Around that time, the news of my twelfth-grade results was flashing; I wasn't worried or depressed about it because I was expecting a good percentage; I had intended that after seeing my numbers, I would get a confidence boost and things would start to be less chaotic, and I would be back on track.

"That wasn't for confidence; that was a validation you were seeking from yourself, as you said, pat on the back, but this time it was you giving yourself that," Sharon says.

I mean, I was still doing good, but I wasn't able to reach my 'full potential', but the chapters I was doing around that time were less problematic and carried less weightage, so I would still be able to do some decent amount of questions, but I wasn't satisfied, and then finally the results came out. The official website of JKBOSE was constantly crashing, and we had to check the merit list; I got all these calls from everybody, which had me developing this sort of faux pressure on me because I couldn't find my result easily, I asked one of my friends to check my score, but I had to fetch my roll number slip which also took a ton of time, I was hysterical all along, and when I was able to get it, the result I saw was not satisfactory. However, I had to put on the same old poker face because I was still in the top 5% of students in the valley, and that alone would be an excellent thing for most people, or should I say "people who are not troubled perfectionists." Everybody in my family and at home was waiting for me to check my result, and I have learned the lesson the hard way that if you don't appreciate your efforts, others sure as hell won't. This result was something I had been really counting on, but what it did instead was drove the last nail in my already ruptured confidence; I had gotten some eighty marks in English after putting all the effort into it, and everyone seemed pleased, but this whole thing wasn't enough for me. Another advisory was out the same day, but this time to reopen the institutes within the next two days.

While searching for my results, I came across Gagan's result; she had a state rank, and to be honest, I felt happy and proud of her; it had made me think that I might also have a state rank of some sort, but needless to say, I was happy for her even after knowing that I don't, but I had a gut feeling that something terrible was about to happen and then it did, she released a press release for Shining Star displaying all the virtues and benefits while she had constantly been telling me that joining that place had been the biggest mistake of her life, I knew how we got those grades and what we did to get them, or what she did to be precise to get those grades because we had always been in contact, I was not late to clear the air because I never wanted any misunderstandings with my friends and, obviously she had been forced and could not have said no.

While I was fully aware and mindful of why I had felt the need to leave Shining Star, she was the same girl who had talked about the reasons she was not going to continue her studies there, but then she had gotten enrolled there, I decided not to think about it because the decision I had taken ultimately didn't feel that bad in hindsight, and then I never felt homesick about that place again.

*****

I reached early and took the front-row seat when I saw some people talking about the results and reminiscing how they had managed to get the numbers of their fate. At the same time, I heard them talking about English paper, and something in me felt like I should talk too, and that would lead to one of the best decisions that I made that year; I added by saying that I got the least marks in English and expressed my grief and then everybody went on how they had not prioritized it and had started preparing for it two days before the test and still managed to get good marks. They were then discussing with each other the topics that Mr. Sarfaraz might potentially teach that day, and one of them added by saying, "I did not attend a single lecture of his because I could never understand a word," I kept interrupting their conversation every once in a while trying to add some value to the conversation, and that is how I made friends, some really great people. The thing is that I am an introvert, but before even knowing it or accepting it, I'd meet people and try to make small talk or add something to the conversation even if it killed me, and then I would feel bad for doing it. It's rare to meet guys who can have reactions more than just based off testosterone, some of my classmates in highschool were cool kids and all about the fun stuff, wouldn't care about grades and things that truly mattered then; it was nobody's fault, but I personally always tried to isolate myself from the madness and impulsivity, hence it never really meant anything other than a casual friendship because according to the Boy-Bible, you must abide by some strict rules some of them including the need to be loud and intimidating in order to make your presence seen, but I never resonated with most of those rules, and then when I met those people at Hikers, I was genuinely happy; they were cool and all, but that didn't stop them from being regulated and serious. The conversation that I had started with one of their group members resulted in me being friends with their whole group, although that's not to say that there were no awkward silences; I mean, I had a tough time, and it's because of all that and being curious I jumped to the conclusion that it . could be because I was just an introvert.

Its later that I found out that it was because I had a processing lag because of how my thoughts were always like a crumpled pieces of papers in rubble, and not just because I was an introvert.

Clearing the doubts or gossiping about the famous couple, we did it together. Although I didn't feel that included at first but whatever inclusion I was getting meant everything, and turns out I was equally included like any of their friends, I had my issues with inclusion.

"There's this one thing that if I'm being asked a question on what am I the happiest about joining Hikers and that course, or that year in general, I will easily say meeting those people, if not the most but one of the most essential and best things. I had never known in my life how it feels to have so many positive people around you who also happen to be boys because, as I said, high school kids always felt like they had to prove a point or

get a grade in the assessment test of that "boy-bible" by not being genuine and by presenting themselves as mean," I say reminiscing.

"Boys can be bitches too. You know people come to me and talk about stuff that is bothering them in their lives, and as we untangle the threads from their past, its rooted in their childhood, but with boys its more severe, the amount of peer-pressure that young guys face is more and everybody just wants to belong somewhere and there's always a price that has to be paid for that, and it is in fact the crippled self-esteem for most of them," Sharon says.

As I was leaving, I got a text from my dad saying that we have a guest at home, he had come after a very long time just because of me so I spent the whole day with him and also because I had made my mind to not mention to any of my relatives that I had enrolled in coaching. It was actually blondie's idea to not tell anyone that you were preparing for an exam to not feel any kind of spotlight pressure. It went on for a couple of weeks; guests would come, and I would have to spend time with them, and I would have to push my schedule and waste time, which led me to frustration; no doubts they were all coming because of my results but celebrating the past while the present was being butchered didn't seem the most brilliant idea to me.

The cult I joined a few years back had an important event lined up, and after posting there on the event day, Heidi and I decided that I would go entirely offline from Instagram to be focused and more attentive.

THE DESCENT INTO ANXIETY

Chapter Four

There's just the right amount of misery you can take and be okay, or at least pretend to be okay with, but when it come from all the directions and at once, it becomes a lot, it gets unbearable, and that's when you try looking for ways out.

As the days passed by, the chapters kept getting more challenging. The exercises kept getting longer and more difficult, sparing me significantly less time to tackle them all resulting in backlogs. The exam was also coming nearer day by day, so I needed to do something about it, and once again, I found myself sacrificing the very thing in my life that supported me throughout the day, sleep. I knew I shouldn't do it, and I had known it from time and time again, but I had never been hooked on the Jee concept before joining Hikers; I never tried to know about it, so I would take almost anybody's advice because I had this skewed idea that everybody knew better than me and I didn't want to be ignorant by not following an advice that anybody would give me, I wanted to do the right things. I had done it again this time when I'd considered Mr. Sarfaraz's advice for sleeping for only four hours.

There's a strange thing about me, I tend to hate it when I feel like I'm putting so much of my time and self into something, it starts to feel like I'm losing myself to it, and that has always been a guiding compass for me to balance my sanity and the studies and so it never seriously impaired my work until this time. I had never wanted this and my subconscious was aware of that; I started sleeping for four hours a night, it took all I had to take that decision, and in the beginning, it didn't feel much so I kept going with it, but I started exhausting myself as the days progressed; I have never in my life had to use that much willpower as I would during those days to get up from the bed after just four hours of sleep still not feeling rested and after it coupled with the difficult sessions I couldn't take it anymore, I'd constantly feel nauseated, groggy and drowsy in the classroom, during the lectures or while interacting with anyone and, I obviously wouldn't get much work done either. At first, I could complete everything, and there would be no backlogs, but then my body physically was telling me otherwise. I stopped making notes once again; I started aching physically, I'd have headaches, I'd feel suffocated, but that wasn't all; I'd wake up and ask myself one question- one consistent question to which I couldn't know the answer, or rather didn't want to answer– "Why am I doing this?" because it had started to take a toll on me and I'd never entertained that, I was denying a part of myself, it was tangling with my compass and it created a sense of dilemma as to why was I even so much invested into it and I would be conflicted all the time.

Every day I would wake up from sleep, sit on the edge of the bed, and ask myself this question, I knew of all possible things I could use as answers, and I would try to do that, but none of it ever made any sense, none of it ever felt the proper or relevant explanation, even though I had enough why's and why not's, they just didn't feel enough, but I kept going with it- every day staying up for twenty hours, waking up with a massive weight of this question tearing me down, not being able to answer it, going along with it, rinse repeat.

My lack of sleep showed in my productivity; I'd doze off during classes. The internet didn't help either – I'd see all these people on the internet who'd talk about how they used to sleep for four hours and "piss in the bowl" and only then – **only being the keyword** – were able to 'crack JEE' while the others were like 'you should stop listening to music', not just during studies but in general because you can end up getting hooked with the lyrics and it might impair your work- but let's be honest that was truth, while I'd do the numerical, and if they were difficult and the music would be on, the only thing I wouldn't do is solve the numerical- so I had to give up on listening to music ultimately, and I did. I hated sacrificing everything that I was sacrificing because of the exam, but I kept doing it and in doing so developing even more contempt for it than before while at the same time losing a part of my self – a tiny bit at a time. I ultimately got tired of my sleep schedule and dumped the whole scene.

Just like any other day, one day, my aunt, my cousin, and my uncle came in to give me "Mubarak," that's what we called congratulating back there. To be very honest, it's always a lot of work when they're home- you have to be really in your senses like you're in a court because anything you say or do can and will be used against you- so it's always exhausting, after everything the conversation directed towards my academics, 'what next?

"Well let me rephrase that because that's not what he said, it was more like, 'this is next for you, and this is how you're going to get it without you having a say in it'"

It's ironic actually because some people think that they have some sort of right to talk about you, comment about you or even take your life decisions even if they have never been part of your highs and lows for the most part, so my father, my cousin, and uncle started discussing which college I was going to take admission into; everybody was just talking and talking and sorting out possibilities for, taking some into account and declining the others while me- the person who had to go to the college every day- was quiet and nobody even happened to consider what I wanted to say about this, remotely. They were filtering potential colleges not based on what I wanted to do in my life, rather than external factors, like how far is it, how badly reputed a particular college was, at one point my uncle made a point to say that, "Nah he's got no chance in that college, he…he won't…noo," referring to an influential but infamous college.

It's kind of strange how everybody tells you to dream big and do this and do that, specifically in Kashmir, be a doctor or engineer, and then if some people dare to, or are in a position to pursue their dreams the same people tell them to stop and be realistic-it *never* made any sense to me, or even in that moment, so I finally spoke up by taking a deep breath in and I said, "Well, we need to go through an examination before getting into the college- it's called Jee- but I'm going to do that next year- I'll take a gap year," and I thought that I was able to shut everybody down but no that's the only thing that didn't happen, it was followed by the questions as to why, what's the reason to that- the questions that I still get asked if I ever meet them again, and then all of a sudden, out of nowhere my cousin said to my dad- not to the person who had to volunteer, to my dad- "Well, he should prepare for a job as well, just like my other cousin will too, he should do that," and a familiar pang that I had felt two years ago was back, that stinging pain along with being indirectly compared to somebody and a tolerance to the belief that my father should make my decision for me- it was ironic once again because my parents were the reason I had taken that particular decision- as if I was some sort of a possession that could be tossed out and stored just the way you want it to, it was violating.

Everybody up to that point had told me to get into jee which I had never wanted but now that I was in it and to get told otherwise was quite frustrating, it was like well I didn't do this 'Jee thingie' because I want it and rather than telling me the same thing that everybody else had you're telling me to do something else, it was confusing, I had gotten comfortable with the routine. However, deep down I still was waiting for that *something* to happen so that I could be spared the misery. And the way everybody had told me about it, the concept of it had been so engraved in me that I felt like my reality was being tested, while inside the hearts of my hearts that's what I had been waiting for, for someone to show up and tell me that I didn't need to go through this madness. Knowing my dad and how easily he can get influenced by any of his relatives or the fact that we'd been in a similar situation two years prior had me panicking because I thought that he might even go ahead with that decision and tell me to not do it, at a much deeper level that's exactly what I wanted but at the same time it was so engraved in me, my vision was so deluded that I thought this was the right thing to do, I was not ready to accept that there are other possibilities, other colleges and career paths.

I was aware that all this was going on in my mind, my dreams had been totally crushed and if that wasn't enough the conversation was now centred around how am I going to travel to the college each day and then my uncle made sure to tell me just the thing that hits the right spot in my body, ones you'd use if you want to paralyse me and haze my mind.

He tells my father, "Hey Waqar, you should really consider teaching him how to ride a bike, poor thing, what's he going to do," and he made sure to side-eye me while saying that and at the same time my cousin was eyeing me too, looking pathetically, and I couldn't say anything because it was the truth that I couldn't, but after having gone through all these whirlwinds from past years I was 'self-aware-enough' to know the place where this was coming from and where to this was headed, it was just another jab, like it always is, to that my initial internal reaction was that I am going to punch this dude right into the face, or at least teach him my boundaries and that he was not successful in making me feel miserable and small, but I knew that anything I'd do would be used against me and now I even have a word, I'd be gaslighted into thinking that indeed I was the one at fault, so I chose not to engage in his bullshit and be a bigger person, I took a deep breath, released it all the way through my nose from deep down my stomach while going through all of this and I smiled through it.

I'd thought that by handling the situation the way I did, I'd been over it, but that was far from being the truth because as I was reading the fifth question of the physics numerical exercise for the seventh time in a row while ruminating about how painful and invasive the encounter had been and the way it had been like this for ages to the point that they don't even think twice before shit-talking about me, I hated myself for having let that happen and I was shaking again while the fact that I had been reading the particular question for Thirty minutes without even trying the slightest to solve it was in the back of my head making it all the worse, and the next thing I know is that I texted Heidi about this, and very rightfully she goes,

"Don't these people have brains? They should be proud that you're taking the most difficult test in India."

At the back of my head was the lingering question, *why am I doing thi*s. And while I knew that I'd regret mourning over the encounter rather than trying to solve the question at hand, I did it nevertheless; I was constantly searching for allies to use as an escape from reality and escape from the weight of the answer to this question. While I was still talking to her I hear someone on the street talking to my dad and just like I knew, he was asking about my career options and what was I going to do- which I hated, I have always hated it- and then during the dinner my father brought the discussion up that that neighbor who was a principal of a government school had suggested that I prepare for a specific exam, he had told my dad, "I believe he can do it," and as my dad was explaining it my gut was already in twists, it's so true that when your purpose is clear and well established, and the foundation of your cause is vital you don't care about the storms to blow everything up and when it's not, even the gentle winds can leave you vulnerable, the same thing was with my decision of taking the Jee test and I knew it, and because of which anything that would make me second guess my decision would feel like a red flag, just like this one, and yeah it also included the part where I had to leave Kashmir to be eligible to finally take on the job- like a pre job training because of which we didn't have to talk about it much as my mom wouldn't let me but the main problem was that I hadn't completely given up on that decision, I didn't feel entirely right to deny that possibility and I kept ruminating about that in the days to come only escalated by the constant chaos of 'why am I doing *this*?'

Chapter Five

Five weeks to go.

The dopamine was coursing through my veins after I had watched a complete series of X-Factor audition videos on YouTube with countless hilarious and ground-breaking performances. It was an extraordinary experience to see the room filled with the laughs and the emotions that the contestants would bring with their performances and sometimes, most of the times, judges losing their mind off laughing hysterically. I hadn't experienced that much joy in a long time and after getting to experience all the raw emotions this was the fifth video I had watched within the same day, but how did I land on it in the first place? Well, I had hopped on to YouTube to learn about the working of a galvanometer where my eyes fell on the thumbnail of a video of judges laughing with no control, seeing the happy faces had brought a smile on my face and brought back the reassurance that I was still capable of feeling good, but the purpose that I had to fulfil of studying a galvanometer had completely escaped my mind just like always; I would see something interesting and follow that while completely losing sight of what I was doing in the first place, but this wasn't always; this was it, only five weeks left for the exams which according to the official notice was going to be held on 24th of April.

There was only so much that I had done because of which everything mattered; the clock was ticking, and every second counted, so I found myself thinking of the ways I could counter all the time that I had not invested in doing the right things, and the only solution that I could come up with was to cut out some sleep hours, and the explanation that I gave myself was … nothing, just because I had to do it. I have always had this thing that when I hear or experience something, it gets encoded in the back of my head, no matter how much I fight it, it's going to manifest over time and show in my behaviour, and this time, it was the advice that Mr. Sarfraz had given earlier in the year; I decided to cut my sleep hours again to four each day and then to feel better I played one more video of highly enthusiastic people having the supernatural courage to show up and audition in front of big record labels and getting their asses whopped. The whole experience was oddly pleasing – it was the only thing that would lighten up my mood and give me an escape from reality, and I found myself doing that again and again.

Following were the days of surviving on four hours of sleep with lots of caffeine, being absent-minded in the classroom, and straining my eyes in the name of keeping them open- often getting called out by teachers for meditating in the classroom, which I would brush off by saying that I was getting suffocated- and watching more audition videos because that's what you do when you're irritated with the task in your hand, your brain starts this thought process of swinging back and forth from past to present to future so you seek out the ways you can avoid that from happening because it's an overall debilitating process- it sucks out all your energy. I would know that I shouldn't be watching any of the videos that I was watching because I would regret when I had to sleep at two at night with more backlogs than I had yesterday, knowing that I have to wake up at six in the morning, but I would still watch them nevertheless as if I couldn't control when I would do it. It isn't that I didn't realize how sleeping less was affecting me- I couldn't do a single question in mathematics- but I continued doing it anyways; it was frustrating; I was wasting my time and spending it unconsciously, and then I was compensating for that by sleeping less which would make me more prone to seek out refuge which would start a chain reaction- I'd be more inclined to distractions, waste more time, and this manifested as procrastination, only this time I was very well aware of it.

****

The exam was approaching, and syllabus was far from completion, and Hikers management kept cancelling our chemistry classes. It reminded me of how this had been the recurring thing in Shining Stars as well, or of the time when Milad had practically begged me over the text message not to leave the coaching by saying, "We can clear all the misunderstandings if you only visit once," But there was nothing to clear, everything was clear as day. The only reason he wanted to clear the misunderstandings was because he wanted to use me as an asset in assigning a JEE selection to the institute's name; that's the only thing he had ever cared about, *obviously*. He texts me, "We have treated you like our children for two years, and is this how you repay that?"

"Textbook manipulator," says Sharon.

But the only thing that came shooting into my brain was how he had humiliated me multiple times over the course without any regard, and been irresponsible and unaccountable for his actions and stupid business choices. He also demanded I call him, which I respectfully denied because I knew he could persuade me over a phone call, and that the same old thing would happen; he'd talk his talk and I'd still be processing what he had said while he'd already moved on to the next thing and I was left speechless and looking dumb.

Once again there was a glimper of doubt about my decision, amplified by the fact that

I had reconnected with one of my friends who still studied in the shining stars and had gotten to know from him that they completed 70% of the syllabus; I thought I had made a terrible mistake of my life, but ultimately it was about self-respect; something that Milad didn't care about, and I hadn't had anyone particularly disrespect me the same way in months at Hikers, so I knew I had taken the right decision to leave that place for good.

"That's gotta be one of the very few times I did something in the name of self-respect, and to the extent that I didn't even think about it again," I say.

"I texted Anirudh and asked him what the hell the Hikers were doing, and also sent him those messages from Milad, and the only thing he did, and was in his control, was to be sorry. Although I felt sorry that he had to be sorry, it developed into a deeper connection – the way he acknowledged my frustration as genuine," I exhale.

Now the only viable option was to tackle a part of the syllabus by myself- inorganic- because Mr. Anirudh had promised to teach the organic using his special method, so there I was cramming the facts from a chapter called 'transition elements' which had seemed simple in twelfth grade but was very far from being one and another guest shows up, and I have to show up yet again. And if this wasn't enough, it was topped with some property dealers coming to see how the house looked from the inside because we had- my Dad- to sell the place, and these visits had become a regular thing now, but this visit was longer than the usual, and after leaving they had asked my Dad to capture a video of everything on the interior and send out to him so that the visits would be less.

I had not liked the concept of selling the house; it was as if everything had been fantastic since we moved into that place, but there was one more facet to it than just this; exhausting the bank accounts and savings for the sake of it, and I had a belief that it would eventually affect my studies – I once had a breakdown because of this in 12th grade– it is at hikers only I found out that you can take a student loan but again why would anybody take out a loan for something they aren't passionate about doing. Besides it was also wasting my time, this whole deal; it is as if every single second, whenever anything would go wrong, I'd want to highlight that I was not taking the test for myself, none of this was for me, and that I had given up on my dreams by taking the decision, but only I didn't do that, so it came out as passive aggression, I had developed a belief system that I should be thanked, since none of it meant anything to me, I had given up responsibility of myself, heck, I didn't even have a sense of responsibility. Whenever my mom would ask me about anything remotely related to my college admission, part of the rage came from the fact that my parents are, in fact, very naïve they'll get influenced by anything anyone says, and she would dig every time, and it had a motto whenever she'd ask, but a part of it came directly from the voice in my head saying that whatever you are doing, it's right because that's what everybody tells you. Better yet, you're doing it for them, so they shouldn't ask questions. You're not obliged to answer their questions and my behavior was very vocal, even if my inner demons numbed me. Morever, my parents never tried to communicate about it which further solidified the belief of me getting exploited in their hands while being alone to process myself and retain my sanity. I felt big and small at the same time. It felt like I was taking so much space but not enough space at the same time.

My Dad comes in with a cell phone; first of all, I let out an exasperated sigh because of how I'd spent two and half hours reading the same line in the said chapter, ruminating about different scenarios that would go down with the selling of the house- none of them beneficial to me - after Mr. Gulzar had left, so I was not very pleased and welcoming to waste another hour recording the video. At first, the video that I shot was high-speed; the other time, it was slow, and the third time, it was very zoomed in; This all made my Dad think that I wasn't taking the video properly and just throwing a tantrum – he expected a 4K cinematic shot which is clearly not possible to get from a budget phone- but the whole time I wanted him to ask me why was I behaving the way I was behaving, maybe I could have told him how I felt about the entire exam ordeal and why I'm acting the way I did, but he didn't, and instead he called me a brat and other things in ten different languages- not that it was his fault, but I was doing that so he would only once ask me what was going on.

As soon as I finished shooting the video I entered my room, and slid down the door after locking it because I felt very lonely and alone- no one was getting me, it felt like everybody wanted something out of me, I had started to believe that I might have a bipolar disorder- clearly because of lack of proper knowledge and extremely short attention span to understand the duration of episodes from the ted-ed video – because of that I felt very lonely it felt like as if I was an animal supposedly a wildlife species kept in a cage my whole life and then suddenly sent into the jungle and discover ways of survival, and the next thing I did was to lay down on my bed and open YouTube and after one long hour of scrolling and watching mindless videos I landed on a YouTube channel it was led by a CA- and the tip she shared was not anything magical or complicated- she was simply suggesting to put down our thoughts on paper if something is stopping us from doing what we must do but there was a problem: journaling wasn't any new concept to me bit when you are overall not contented with yourself and your life you even stop trying so I thought it was futile but I still kept watching other videos from her and the next thing I know is that I had watched all of her videos. The way she spoke with all the experience she had gained in her journey felt very appealing so after spending another two hours watching her videos I decided to make a plan to study because obviously the exam was right in the corner and I was aware of that. With all the time I had left I roughly assigned a certain number of hours to each chapter, and knowing the length of each chapter I wasn't doing justice to any of them but the deeply rooted perfectionist in me wouldn't let go of this ignorance and wanted to cover every single thing. Over the next few days, I tossed and turned, following some of the parts of the schedule, disgusted by the miserable life I was living and hated doing other facets of it– usually the difficult ones.

One day while Mr. Anirudh and I were discussing about the syllabus and the difficulty of the paper, I heard a voice in my head which told me that I should have a deeper career conversation with him. He was not the type of guy who only cared for money, he was a big sucker for respect too-for it had been a harsh comment from the Hikers management that had made him to decide to leave it- he wanted all of us to grow in a sense that was true to us. I felt like I should ask an opinion from him about what I had intended to do in order to be successful and I felt like I wanted to tell him my plans and that it was all a façade and I didn't give two shits about the exam, but before I could say anything the bell rang and he had some pre-occupation and just like that he left and a part of me that had gotten its hopes up and wanted to have a serious conversation and get candid about my likes, dislikes, motivations and inspirations in taking this test or fulfilling the higher purpose in my life faded away just as he faded away when the doors of the elevator shut together.

The number of hours I had assigned to each chapter were already dwindling, and I was still surviving on four hours of sleep every day. Somewhere along the line, I started searching for the song that I had come across while watching those talent show performances namely 'fight song' There was one more song by the same artist called 'Stand by You' The problem that I supposed to be doing was already dreading so the idea of listening to this new song didn't feel bad so I went with it.

I couldn't make out the song's lyrics at first, so I looked up the lyrics while I played the song for the second time. It is as if the lyrics spoke to me. Although it was a song written from a partner's perspective in a relationship, I dedicated those lyrics to myself as a shoulder to cry on. I was dedicating this song to myself, consoling myself because, as the lyrics read,

"Even if you can't find heaven, I'll walk through hell with you; love, you're not alone. I'm going to stand by you,"

Because this was the hell, and all I could do was stand by myself because nobody else seemed to do that for me. Somewhere along the line, I stopped texting Heidi over little things and acting like a baby because I couldn't sift through what I was going through and what I was feeling, so explaining it to someone virtually was a big deal, and as I unpacked the lyrics of this song it was as if I had wrapped an arm around myself and I knew that I was all alone, but I also knew that I was enough to be there for myself. As I was hearing Rachel's – the artist's- voice get pitchy towards, "I'll walk through hell with you," a new stream of tears would flow from my eyes as I could resonate with that pain and sense it as I was reflecting on every single thing that I had done that year and not taken myself into the consideration. I was being sorry for myself. And if I hadn't cried like a baby already, I started playing the song 'who says.' The lyric in that song, "Who says you don't pass the test," always hits the right buttons along with other things that she says in the song. After listening to these songs for some time, letting myself experience all the suffering I was going through, and just allowing all the emotions to flow, I felt a sense of calm and relief. I knew what I had to do next. It all started with the reforming and deforming of my schedule to fit six hours of sleep from four hours, and as if there had been a pent-up breath in my lungs and all I had been doing was the superficial work of not letting that air flow through my nostrils, all along; it finally did, and I smiled for the first time with all my heart in months.

It was such a cathartic experience for me.

Chapter Six

I had always thought I would get more in touch with my spiritual self after I pass tenth-grade. I used to think that I would only have to study the subjects that I was passionate about because I always had a way to work around those subjects. I would attend a lecture from my teacher in science and I would remember that for days or even a year, and I would get to continue doing my research which I had stopped because of the tenth grade. Although it was still at the back of my head because one time I was studying the transportation in plants and I also had studied the contraction and relaxation of lungs in respiration and I observed that there was a correlation of pressure with the volume but I couldn't know if that made any sense because the coaching was closed so that we could prepare well, hence I couldn't ask Jamshed sir.

"What was I saying again?" I ask.
"You were about to tell me about your spiritual self."
"Oh yeah, right."

….But it had become the total opposite as in I had started to reduce the amount of time I'd spent praying during Ramadan substantially.

Ramadan was approaching and we got a call from my aunt saying my cousin and Irtiqa had a baby boy and we had to show up at the hospital righteously, and a few days leading to that day my cousin organized a massive party on baby's birth, we had to be there.

Murshid came to pick me and my dad while my mom was already there, we had to stop on our way at a bakery shop because it was six in the morning and everybody had to do their breakfast.

Murshid killed the engine and parked the car on the roadside because it would come in handy. Me along with my dad got out of the vehicle; I with three handbags and a backpack with books in it with me, and as we were walking I entered the lane next to the one that I was supposed to- the one that leads to me to my aunt- as soon as I emerge out of that lane realizing that it had been the wrong lane and feeling pathetic for my state but brushing it off because it didn't feel like a big deal as I had grown accustomed to zoning out and do out of order things; but my dad and Murshid started laughing their butts off in the middle of the street as if I had put on a clown show, one that I clearly wasn't aware of.

We entered my aunt's place and the next thing you know is Murshid telling everybody about the stupid situation and my dad was also involved in the fun making process. It was pretty strange; I hadn't taken it as that big of a deal but Murshid had thought of it it as hilarious, and my dad was just going with it. I felt like punching Murshid in his fucking face as he proceeded to make sure to tell everybody about it which made them look at me with the eyes they always do that makes me feel like an unfortunate soul.

Was it because I didn't know the way to my aunt's house? No, I had been to that place for like million times; it was not that I had forgotten, but my mind was completely occupied; I was not mindful and present at the moment and I had zoned out.

I can't say I exactly had fun that day, we slaughtered some sheep and a cake; distributed the former in the neighbourhood, ate lunch and then had snacks and then had dinner and my cousin Kareem dropped us home.

We woke up in the middle of the night to eat our meals and hydrate ourselves for we couldn't eat anything for the rest of the day – we were fasting, the Ramadan had started. When we were done with all the eating and prayers my parents went to sleep but I didn't, I decided to take on the question from the coordination chemistry from the extra class that I had recently started to attend from the other section of the JEE students which also gave me a reason to ditch my physics and mathematics class.

This went on for a couple of days till I got exhausted of it; waking up in the middle of the night, sleeping poorly, brainstorming all day long about the questions and at the same time not being able to pay attention regularly. I had also started to do this Hawaiian exercise called Ho'oponopono prayer, it comprised of letting go of things, being grateful for things, asking for forgiveness and spreading love. It was like a daily affirmation and I had downloaded it on my phone. I would Tune in to it while studying in the study room facility of hikers.

I then one day after feeling torn finally decided that I was going to prioritize my mental well-being because it had once again started to affect me physically I couldn't care less about the fact that exam was in 15 days and I had to had a huge chunk of syllabus to cover rather something shifted in my mindset driven by the lack of my religious fulfillment and discovering that girl talk about "having something that makes you feel grounded " and I had this sudden burst of optimism that everything was going to be alright, but at the core what I was really thinking was that I don't care what happens; I'm in distress. I made another schedule comprising of "me time" and prayer time and around thirteen hours of study time once again just like a perfect schedule.

I decided that I was going to direct my attention on the subjects – better yet, a subject- that I was relatively better at which is chemistry and I thought that I'd tackle the other subjects later, the difficult ones that require a lot of analytical thinking. I had officially ditched the other two subjects.

And then one night a miracle happened. We woke up at night as a part of the habbit to eat sahur and I casually made a point to check telegram – something that I wouldn't usually do. I saw texts from many of my friends and I didn't know what to expect. I clicked on one of the profile and what I saw was about to change the course of the next three months, or should I say my whole life.

There was a circular- an official NTA notice- which were clear that the JEE 2022 exams have been postponed by a two-month period.

Now, I have a tendency to have a breakdown on miniscule things sometimes while other times even the news headlines don't do a thing to me. So, I didn't feel much at the moment. At first I thought I was dreaming because hey, at the end of the day, it was still night time, so I got up and made myself sit straight, adjusted my posture.

I clicked on all the unread messages and they all seemed to say the same thing that the JEE 2022 exams had been postponed on account of rising COVID cases. I couldn't believe what I saw – it felt like my dreams and manifestation had come true- I couldn't contain myself anymore and I replied Thank God in inverted commas to all the texts and the excitement in my eyes was clear as the day which caught my parent's attention and I blurted the news.

I had not felt that happy in days. Giving myself the time to work on my mental well-being and feeding my soul had worked, it felt like doing the Ho'oponopono prayer had helped too so I thought what better than to continue doing it.

I couldn't help myself but stayed up till the morning making a plan for the next two months. I remember thinking to myself, "You were determined to do it when you had only fifteen days left and now see you have almost two and half months to do it; You are ready. You can do this. Let's do this," and of course I scheduled chemistry first and then physics and math respectively. This is not to say that the plan that I made I executed it the way I had planned to; there were days when I'd spent entire hours editing the plan, transforming it; but that was all the part of the process.

"I'd sometimes get frustrated because of all that planning but it was later in the life that I realized that planning and planning more and failing at it but planning even more, planning every second was a part of me being myself and the only choice that I had was to accept myself for it. I wanted to live a spontaneous life but I knew if I would get too tempted I'd end up wrecking everything," I say.

I spend next two days feeling exhilarated and euphoric- I went on a shopping spree- I ordered some hair products a pair of sneakers, a watch, some clothes, a new backpack and a bottle of water. A text that I had sent Heidi read, "When I'm done with the exam I'm going to get myself all of those things," but I realized that I couldn't keep my life at a standstill so I ended up buying it all.

I spent the Ramadan going on and off on fasting, I practiced the prayers and I did the

Ho'oponopono, I'd study with that playing in the background I was spending time on myself it made me feel like I existed. It made me feel grounded, it made me feel less like an object and that I had a life. I'd watch Ted-Talks in my free time, I started journaling again I would study and be mindful and I'd spent most of the time intentionally. I'd revise and by the end of the Ramadan the major part of the chemistry was done, once again my life was great; I remember thinking to myself that the feeling of being depressed hopeless and helpless that I had experienced just a couple of weeks ago was stupid: but little did I know that I was denying the fact that I was running away from the problems not facing them, heck I even thought that the problems that I had faced in 11th grade and giving it the name of depression had been silly and weak. It was two days before Eid that things started to change once again. There's a thing about mental health well-being, you just know it in your gut when something goes wrong or is about to go wrong, it's just a matter of time and being non-ignorant about accepting it. The same was happening with me.

One day I had forgotten my earphones at home and the theoretical part of the chemistry was over, I had to do the sums in a physical chemistry chapter and without my headphones I started to freak out I couldn't concentrate or retain my focus. I kept looking away from my cubicle while the beads of sweat started forming near my hairline on the forehead. It felt like a panic attack as I realized that I had only done twelve questions in an hour, one third of what I'd normally do but I questioned myself that what possibly could trigger a panic attack– it wasn't that big of a deal, while at the same time I felt warm and I felt like my heart had been filled with an abundance of oxygen and I needed to exhale a million times in a second or otherwise my head would meet the frequency of the veins in my head and the sound in my ears and eventually explode, it felt like my head and ears had a heart of their own that was beating with a million Hertz frequency. I had not experienced this in over a month which meant I'd forgotten how to cope with it, I'd forgotten how it felt like. Thoughts like how am I going to perform in the exam if I go through something like this while solving the sum, how am I going to manage the time if I keep going at the pace of twelve *numericals* an hour. Am I going to experience a panic attack in the middle of my exam just like I did in the 11th grade? And I immediately closed the book, took out my phone and started scrolling YouTube so that I could shut this noise.

I got home and after lunch, yes lunch because id stopped fasting as there was a lot going on whether I acknowledged it or not, I made a point to write down all the tasks that I needed to complete before Eid so that I could enjoy the holidays, only to discover that for the next two days I couldn't be productive I'd get nothing done I knew there was a lot that I needed to do but at the same time I couldn't do it. I just did not have energy to do it I kept telling myself that I don't feel depressed; but I couldn't make myself to study either and then I gave up and decided that one extra day of holiday wouldn't hurt, after all the major portion of chemistry was done and I spend the rest of the day listening to music after I had restrained myself from it for a month hyper fixating.

THE FALSE FAÇADE OF SUCCESS

Chapter Seven

I woke up around three thirty in the morning just like I always would on the day of Eid. I took a long shower and dressed into a 'Khan Dress' and offered my morning prayer and after that we had our morning Kehwa, although I didn't feel qualified to drink it because I hadn't been fasting but I did it anyways. After a complete month of fasting we Muslims on the day of Eid before having anything else early in the morning drink something sweet as a form of indication that we have accomplished a full month of fasting for the year, for good.

I alongside my dad rushed to Eidgah (a place where we all gather and pray and express our gratitude for being able to fast and getting rid of our sins, and expressing our happiness about it) for the Eid prayer and luckily we got a decent seat; It was nice to see everybody dressed in the Shalwar-Kameez, or any other form of new clothing, gathered together to perform a common obligation, offering the Eid prayer, but what I had not realized was that I had stepped foot in a mosque after two years. Yes, I had not been to a mosque in over two years it had started because of the COVID lockdown that followed two years of me feeling desolated and disconnected. I had not spoken to anyone in two years – by anyone I mean a stranger- I had not seen a new human face in the last two years, I felt disconnected to my soul and my faith. In the room of all those people I felt lonely. Surely I tried to reassure myself that it had been because of covid but I couldn't seem to please my inner conscience with that answer. My inner demons pointed towards the fact that even after doing all of this being determined with my studies I still sucked I had nearly failed 11th grade I busted my ass but the results were crappy in the 12th grade and had it not been the exam delay I'd fail JEE with no questions asked.

And then the omens part of me kicked in and begin to tell me that all of this unfortunate happened because I had stopped going to the mosque and praying, it felt like my life could get back in order if I started, once again, to offer my prayers in the mosque but what I didn't realize was that rather than finding out the real problem and doing something about it this was my attempt put the blame on something so that I could free myself of it, I was using religion and faith as a defence mechanism. While hearing the sermon muffled with the voices in my head I all of a sudden started to sob starting with the blurry vision of the tear falling down from the corner of my eye to full blown crying, but I did manage to remain quiet and it was around the same time that we make dua'. I raised my hand and asked for... well nothing. I didn't know what to ask for which triggered a part of me that I had done a phenomenal job at supressing...

and I started crying even more, so much so that I had to cup both sides of my face with my hands. I wanted to make a dua but I didn't know what to ask; Or maybe I wasn't ready to bear what I would ask for. Sure, I was preparing for an Exam and I would make a dua about it, but I didn't do that. The same question that had been a lingering part in the back of my head came shooting back, "why am I doing this? Why am I taking this test?" why should I pray that I qualify this test even though I don't want to. Heck, I couldn't even ask for a better health because deep down, I knew that the first and the major step towards the betterment of health would come, only and only if I get rid of this exam for good, but how could I do that? How could I not take the sacred test? By this time I had started to internalize the belief that I have bipolar disorder; The way I'd have some great days followed by the terrible ones. So, I cried for that too – "why me?" What did I do to have bipolar disorder escalated with the Mumbles and cries of the crowd as they were asking for something they desperately wanted, my nose started to become fluid thank God I had a face mask on, I took out a handkerchief and blew my nose as gently as I could so I wouldn't disgust the people surrounding me but when I realized that "dua session" was about to finish and we had to get up and get in the horizontal lines – called *safas* in order to offer our prayers, I made a Dua that "whatever happens in my life should lead to good things, whatever it be" and just like that we all stood up people who were around me were looking at me, my teary eyes and red face, but I didn't feel any shame, I didn't get embarrassed, I had already failed at my whole life and now I was blowing the only strong suite of my life too, academia; Nothing mattered anymore.

We left the Masjid and I remember feeling euphoric and the omens part rose from the ashes of logic like a phoenix displaying that it was because I had visited the mosque and offered a prayer, and I should do it more often, without any regard for the fact that my brain was messed up and I'd have been made to stay in a mental health facility if I'd seen a medical professional.

I spent the first two days on the Internet because like always I had no plans. I was supposed to feel good and rest, but I was conflicted and not at ease I installed Clash of Clans and played for some time, listened to music; but my holiday was going nowhere, all I kept thinking about was the items on my To Do List. Later in the evening, I reconnected with my friends on Instagram after I had blacked out on all my socials they were all asking the same thing that where the hell had I been. I told them about my mental health struggles while all of them began to console me by saying that everything is going to be alright well, one of them even suggested that I should regularly talk to them, in order to have a social connection, which in hindsight I should have done. I reassured every one of them that things were finally alright and then that there was nothing to worry about.

I landed on this YouTube video about burnout, I had not heard of it before that moment so I didn't know it existed I also ended up watching a ted-ed video on bipolar disorder and, well, I concluded I did not have bipolar disorder. And I had a name to what I was feeling –burnout- I tried implementing the tips and tricks that the speaker shared to counter the burnout but it was already the second day of Eid; End of my holiday but I took another day off anyway.

Chapter Eight.

It's always been difficult for me to bounce back from holidays; Let alone an unresolved burnout, I tried picking up the pace and finished my chemistry entirely, although the entire organic section was still pending.

The next thing I had planned to do was to do physics and it started with downloading the revision one shot videos and notes from the YouTube- obviously because of the Internet- and scheduled them throughout the month of May.

We had finally started doing organic chemistry. Mr. Anirudh decided to leave the hikers, and about three hundred people were in shock for how he could quit like that after promising the syllabus completion using his special tips and formulas. How could he just run away like that?

So, he didn't. He made a promise, although all of us were hazed and just wanted a slither of hope that we couldn't see that it was impossible to complete that much syllabus in the days that we had left; he conducted extra classes and doubt sessions so that nobody would face a problem. We ended up making a telegram group chat so that we could continue our classes. After that day I stopped attending the coaching I would watch those physics one shot videos – the key word being *watch*- I'd follow along the steps as the educator solved the questions on the other end of the internet. I didn't realize that I should have been the one practicing along with those *numericals* or it was just a way of denying the fact that actually solving them horrified me to my core, so I was pretending that I was okay with it by not addressing the elephant in the room.

The visits from property dealers to home didn't stop until we found a buyer for our home, but it didn't stop there, the next thing on the list was to look for a house to buy where we'd move to. It comprised of paying visits to hundred million houses, although I visited only a few of them, and then the series of discussions where we'd untangle every single facet for buying a particular property, but we couldn't shortlist a place so we ended up selecting a piece of land in the outside of the countryside.

As much as I tried to distance myself from any of this I found myself getting more and more sucked into it. Nevertheless, I was going to live there while the exam would be over within a couple of weeks, and it was my parents hard earned money so I had to intervene. I became a part of those discussions so much so that I'd sometimes spend entire hours with it and not study.

I didn't realise that subconsciously I was using it as an excuse to not study, or it was really a reason that I couldn't study because it was distracting but at the end of the day it showed in my learning process. And when we did finally decide to buy that piece of land it came with lots of technical jargon which was obviously a problem because dad seems to hate new things; He gets overwhelmed by change, and honestly so do I or, or I used to, I'd rather say.

Around the same time a brewing conflict within our family turned into a full blown feud it felt like we would lose the only loyal relatives that we had because we were put on a crossroad, which didn't help. My mom would be depressed and anxious and she wanted me to talk to her and console her which I found myself doing very often, I inevitably had to become a part of all the gossip, but I was also on a tight schedule- I shouldn't have wasted time but shouldn't and don't always align because what I did do ultimately led to me having less and less time for preparation and tweaking my plan even further. And whatever time I had assigned as "self-time" turned into me packing stuff for we were moving, which was hectic and exhausting; its never easy to move, my dad didn't seem to realize that. But what I find fascinating is that, my dad wouldn't also object me for helping with the packing as if it was my duty (which it was) but at the same time I wasn't doing what I was doing because I liked it, so whose fault was it that I was trapped? I had planned to pack my stuff after the exams, but my mind had something else to say, I found it fascinating and novel and hey, I had lived in that house for six years, I had spent my most blissful and terrible years of life there, of course I loved it, and let's just say that it took my mind away from the reality. No doubts I'd do it in my free time, it still helped with the overall productivity and now I understand that giving yourself time to rest and reboot also adds up as a productive move.

But once again, I had compiled back logs, and I needed to get rid of them to save my what seemed to be the *perfect plan.*

I had finally completed the physics – or so I thought- and I had decided to take the dreaded mock test. There were two resistances to taking a mock test: I would freak out- the real reason, and I always seemed to have more important things to do like revise whenever I'd think of a mock test. I sat down with a timer on and logged into the official NTA websites for mock tests but it was irresponsive so I had to opt for a private app- which may or may not have shown me the relevant questions. Be it a mock test or not, at the core of it, I was still solving the sums, I still went into the flight and fight mode the way my body would become hot and I'd start getting out of breath, but the fact that my exam was within next twenty days, I tried to handle myself with as much grace as I could. Even reading the questions was difficult, let alone solving them. Some questions were completely irrelevant, or so I thought based on what we'd studied because at the back of my head were the voices telling me that I have not done enough, I have not studied enough, and whatever has been taught to you is incomplete and not the part of the bigger picture. And out of all the questions that seemed relevant; some I couldn't solve, and the other ones I didn't remember the formulas to solve. "After all, it's been like a week or something since I last revised this," I remember saying to myself. The idea of a perfect revision hadn't still changed even after three years of tenth grade, I still needed to revise everything in one sitting and at most five days before the test to retain the information. As I kept switching and sifting through questions, I realised I had forgotten everything. I evaluated the test and got around 82%ile which if you know is a failure in JEE. I texted Heidi and told her that I had finally taken the damned mock test and I told her about my 82%ile; at first she was very happy with it, and then I had to break it to her that it meant near failure to which she replied by saying that I should do better. I said to her that it was because of not revising I had forgotten the formulas and that if I take the test after proper revisions, I'd remember them and I'd do better in the test. Once again, I used revision as a way to get away with the mock test. I faced a dilemma, or maybe it was just a charade of trying to keep my sanity and avoiding the truth to prevent the mental damage, that should I be doing the revisions or taking the mock tests because mock tests were showing me the reality that it was not just the matter of revise, I also didn't know anything at all. I couldn't decide what to do, and I didn't, I closed my books and went for an hour long break because I needed an hour to recover from the test, because the worst part was that I always had a problem while solving the sums but I'd always mask it which made it even worse. I came back and texted Heidi that I was going to start doing Mathematics from 4th June, to which she replied by saying that, "You're one intelligent ass, I know you're going to make it," because I had told her that I was freaking out, for it was the first time in my life I had to take a test that comprised of more than Fifty chapters, I kept thinking to myself that I was going to forget everything on the exam day.

I took another test, the next day and the same thing happened, I didn't remember what I'd learned, and the rest of it was new. And I ended up deciding that I wasn't going to take any mock tests and direct all my attention in doing mathematics because the real result of mock test was that I had forgotten whatever little I had learned, but it was not a problem, I just had to revise everything once before taking a test, and I don't know why but seeing those numbers somehow mattered that I completely stopped in a way to stop getting hurt.

For the next couple of days I attempted to learn mathematics, just a couple of Chapter's would be enough, while at the same time being conflicted because I'd also have to do the revision to secure whatever I'd already learned. I tried giving it my all but I couldn't do it.

"One of the worse outcome of these coaching institutes was imposter syndrome. They would constantly remind all of us of how we weren't shit, or anything special. I mean reality checks are good, but in hindsight I was wired differently, and they would prove to be counterproductive. Doing good in mathematics, and then messing up but doing great again in twelfth grade made me believe that I could actually do it, but then going into the Hikers, and how debilitating I was towards myself, I lost sight of who I was, people who I used to talk with on daily basis would do good in the mentioned subject, and I would only notice that without any regards to the fact that all along I had not been taught that subject the

same way these guys were. I even had a self-testimony of Mr. Maher saying the same. It got to a point where I didn't know what was real anymore later down the line, mathematics had become a major part of my personality, and then even dropping it didn't feel good, I started to question if anything about me had ever been real and legitimate. I was devastated because it had been my favourite subject and all I kept telling myself was "You've chosen this. You've chosen this life, this stream, it's your favourite, your body and mind is lying to you," so I kept going, lying to myself, escalated by the message that media gives you to torture yourself in the name of success.

"The biggest mistake of my life was thinking that the only career choice was to pursue the subjects that I loved, which I later realized after going through a ton of turmoil that it does not have to be true. You can love a particular subject, and it can feel like an equal of soul mate to you; you're passionate about it but you don't necessarily need to have a career in it. And

what was worse was that I used to feel guilty thinking that I wouldn't pursue my career in the subjects that I was passionate about, but it was only later I realised that there's no point in feeling guilty or shame, because no matter what I would do in life those subjects would always have a dear place in my heart and it had always been real with no arguments."

I thought to take a break from it and do physics revision instead, only to realise that I didn't just have to revise it but rather start from the scratch, just like always, but this time it was an even bigger problem because I had not solved the *numericals* in the first place, this was the first time I was doing it. The exam was in twelve days and I still had chemistry to revise, so, the only viable option that I saw was to compensate, by sleeping less. Just a few days ago Heidi had suggested that I should work at night as well to which I had replied by saying, "I'm scared to do it, it doesn't end well," and "I can't keep myself awake," and she had suggested me to drink coffee, and I had told her, "It burns my stomach, I can't," and yet, there I was planning to adapt the ultimate doom of my life.

"In hindsight, it came from a place of valuing an exam more than myself and my health because of which I kept doing it again and again," I say.

June 9th, 2022.

I had come back from the mosque after offering the Friday prayer and we were having our lunch when my dad got a notification, he opened it and it was the interior plan of the house that we were going to build on the piece of land that we had bought. It was followed by a text message which read, "Take a look at this plan and do tell us if you feel like tweaking something." We finished our Lunch at light speed, because I found it exciting and hopped on to my dad's phone to discuss the plan. My mom and I decided that there were going to be a couple of tweaks and I edited it on my desktop, thinking that those would be considered. What I was experiencing was true joy and excitement, I was getting to be able to plan the interior of the house that we we're going to live in, I had not felt that giddy in a long time, but what I didn't realise was that it would make me as excited that studies would completely escape my mind, because that's what happened. I developed an obsession towards that home plan over next few days and it was the only thing that was on my mind. I'd imagine how it was going to turn out, what thing was going to be placed where, and I just couldn't get enough of it. But my brain didn't just stop there, my day dreaming – Which I didn't call it back then- got even bizarre, I started thinking of home plans in general, the interior designs, the colors, the accents, what would complement what in a house, and that would be the only thing on my mind, and I'd have to -every single day- sleep with a regret that I couldn't complete my tasks, and clearly had to do something about it. *But did I?*

June 13th, 2022.

I had opened YouTube for a query where I had landed on this YouTube video from an educator, at first glance I thought it was going to be just another "do these questions and you have a guaranteed percentile" videos but I watched it anyways- it had become a second nature to me- but for the first time the video was not about it. The video was uploaded by a channel named "Mathongo," where the educator was addressing the mental and emotional state of the aspirants, or at least say a couple things about it, really just a bare minimum but even that was fascinating then, in that state. He suggested that all we needed to do was to shake it off, and not try to do anything new, and have faith in ourselves for whatever we had done and revise it- I don't know what it did to me; was it the way he had said it, or the timing, or just the fact that nobody was home and I could just cry out everything that was pent up in me- which also had become a second nature, I was going through a lot of emotional and mental turmoil but apparently it was normal and addressing the elephant in the room would somehow lead to demotivation, I would ignore it, and then I had to have these crying sessions when my Mental container would be filled to the brim- and the only thing that kept coming into my head was that I was going to fail, I was doomed, and I didn't deserve to qualify this test, heightened by the fact that the last few days, or, better yet, weeks had been waste one way or another. I plugged in my headphones and started listening to the song 'Fight back' 'Stand by you' and 'Who says' and all I did was to cry. I was exhausted. I had had enough. I didn't have it in me to keep fighting, but I knew I still had to do it.

I hereby announce that I did whatever I could have had done for this exam. I worked hard, smartly. Trying new things, got rejected and then felt dejected; tried it again. I woke up for so many nights abandoned Instagram, music. Prepared myself to take this exam. Accepted my flaws and tried to work on them. Got sick, took days off and started again. Got distracted but each time I started again. Experienced a complete mental breakdown, several times and

moved on. Met new people with new taste, treated them well, messed some friendships, learned new things got out of my comfort zone and moved on figured out my future figured out that we were moving out, attended so many guests and people who came to visit to buy this place.

I wasted time, definitely, yes, I did, but I did those things that I never thought I would, or I had ever done.

What do I worry about and why do I worry about it?

I have done whatever I could, rest is in the hands of almighty. Indeed he has something special planned for me.

At the end I pray that my exams postpone just a little bit and that I get selected in the state NIT atleast. In sha allah. Basically, even deciding to go for it, JEE mains 2022, getting an admission at coaching, taking the course, and sitting in the lecture hall, filling the forms, these all are the biggest steps that I have taken this year. Then preparing for so long even if I

wasn't mentally stable for even a single minute.

I am not kidding, not a single minute!!

And even sometimes sleeping less.

"My journal entry from that day."

"Now that I think of it that the song Who Says became irrelevant because, it was no one other than me who was telling me that I wasn't enough, I had stopped caring about people's opinions and it was me degrading myself."

We had accomplished organic chemistry just a week ago as promised using Anirudh's special method, and the only thing left to do was to do the practice questions, and for short cut method, I seemed to be doing pretty great. Organic chemistry had been the major stressor and hope at the same time for us; for it was the last section in chemistry that we did, and the major part of the chemistry would come from this section, but we did leave out some subtopics as they were 'less important,' and didn't have much chance of being asked in the exam. Just like any other day I was doing Organic chemistry questions at the rate of twenty-two questions in an hour, when I hear a thud at my door, followed by another which turned into a full on knocking, I opened it and saw my dad, obviously. But this time he was there for more than just peeping out of the window, but I didn't know that, and one thing that I had been able to do within last two years was to establish my boundaries during studies, so I made a disgusted face on purpose in an attempt to make him known that he had interrupted my quality study time, and I asked hurriedly what was the problem. He had dropped his phone in water, and now he wanted me to check it because it had stopped working. I don't know what he thought, or why he thought that, he suddenly called me obnoxious and said that my face looked like as if there had been a slaughter of hundreds of pigs on it. It happened very quickly so I couldn't capture the place where that had come from, he had dropped his phone, he interrupted my study time, he had been the one for all the disturbances that I had to bear with because of getting the word out for the sale of our house, and now he was giving me the attitude. I stayed calm, and I didn't say anything. This had started two years ago, I'd stop responding to anything hateful he'd say, and justify it by saying that he's had his fair share of trauma in life and that was why he behaves this way, and just like that things would be over as if nothing had had happened. But I didn't seem to go with that mind-set that day, I retaliated by asking where had that come from, and he started talking nonsense thinking that he was making any sense, but all I could think of was that he had interrupted my state of focus, and he had dropped his phone in the water, but my life had turned into various directions that I wasn't in the mental capacity to say anything more, I knew it wasn't my fault but I just wanted to cry, cool thing is that I somehow was able to contain myself and be calm. Turns out my uncle – his younger brother- had said something to him over the phone, but that still didn't rationalize the bitchy behaviour towards me, like why do I care, and what the hell is my fault if your relatives like to mess with you, deal with your emotions like an adult, rather than act out of them like a two year old?

"Sorry to break it to you, but that could be Generalised anxiety you know? You said it yourself, you had not been responding to whatever he'd tell you, and then he'd got tired of it and had wanted an outlet. It's highly likely, at the core it is insecurity too but some of us are not in tune with that and by seeking out these repulsive behaviours, we feel a sense of calm in the chaos and uncertainty that we create in our heads," Sharon tells me.

"Umm... whoa ... that was a lot of ...uh... technical jargon to take in," I say but I'm not baffled.

"Well, you might not like to hear it but it is what it is, and as a therapist it is my job to tell you all of the possibilities," she says while leaning back in her chair and covering her head with her arm. *"Or it could be because of an underlying issue,*

because I can see the pattern here," she adds.

I reverted my attention back to studying after the whole thing but I couldn't focus and what he had called me kept shooting back into my head whenever I'd start to read a new question. I didn't understand what my fault was so I kept ruminating about it. Just a night before this, I'd gotten to know my exam dates, and my exam was on the sixth day of the scheduled date. Basically, they release a list of dates and everybody's exam is distributed throughout those dates, because there's great amount of crowd. I had manifested and prayed for this, and a new ray of hope had been arisen for me to do better. I went downstairs to make myself some noodles to eat so that I could cheer up myself and feel better, because of all the ted talks I had watched, I'd also watched the one that teaches you to "Choose your happiness, and create your own version of happiness," and the idea that when you're feeling down, you should make an effort to cheer yourself up. But to my luck, apparently all the utensils that I could use to make noodles were occupied or been packed, so no noodles which didn't help anything. I got back in my room upstairs and I knew that the last thing that I could do was to study, so I thought what best thing to do then watch something fun online. I tuned into the high school musical, 'Victorious,' I had watched some snippets leading to that event and had found them hilarious. I kept watching one episode after the other and before I knew it was the lunch time.

After having my lunch, I watched it again, I completed the whole season that day and did nothing. It numbed my brain to stop thinking of what had happened earlier but also wasted my time.

I spent the first half of the next day the same way before I knew I had to do something about it. In an attempt to make things right, I planned to reduce my sleep schedule to four hours.

"Oh my god! Not again," Sharon *exclaims out of frustration which is clear from her face which is understandable, wasn't that understandable then.*

"I know at this point, this must sound boring but trust me, even after I knew it wasn't healthy, I Just couldn't understand but this used to be like my backup plan, and each time it would lead to terrible things," I reply.

By this time I'd already started to get puffy eyes but it wasn't bad and then it did get bad when I planned to wake up all night that night to study, which I obviously didn't do, and the reason? I kept dozing off, and then throughout the day I'd feel sleepy. This went on for a few days till I couldn't take it, and you might ask, the timetable was in ruins, but by this time I'd made a decision that I was going to leave out mathematics entirely-Mr. Maher had told us that he'd done the same thing- and then I got sick. My eyes started to hurt so I couldn't stay up at nights, my stomach was hurting badly so no coffee for me, and a terrible stinging headache and I had to stop doing anything at all. Mathematics was out of the equation and now the number of revisions would also suffer.

20th June, 2022.

I have not been working for quite a lot of days and I feel stuck.

I watched Victorious, got pain in my eye had to take a day off and then so on UGHHH! I'm not going in exact detail but today I took a day off because my stomach was hurting bad I haven't even tried to study today I don't know why and I wasted like two more days after the announcement of exam date it kind of feels like I'm sabotaging myself I thought I'd do two more revisions but now I only have time for just one but I may somehow manage to cope up with this by staying up for some nights. Why am I doing that? Because I've watched victorious last week and I wasted time, I'm trying to compensate which I know is undoubtedly horrible.

I'm having such a stupid stomach ache these days that I cannot even drink coffee to stay awake at night. I feel like time is slipping out of my hands and I know 'me' is the only one to be held responsible for all of this and I do know that but somehow I'm not fulfilling my responsibilities from quite some days and this is becoming a self-sabotage for me. You know what I have made like four strategies in the last four days and I don't even want to lift a pen and paper to write my plans anymore, there are insane number of people out there who are going to tell me that it's all your fault and you should have had worked harder, you stupid ass!

I know that's why I'm not using those phrases here because I know I'm suffering from a lot of mental health issues and me being one of my own triggers is the last thing that I would want to do.

Now I know I wasted my time but the point is that I know how precious my time is and I want to save it and use it judiciously but I'm not doing it and which is a sign enough for me to say that there's something wrong and I'm definitely not able to figure it out you know, like, Can you believe me? Yesterday at this exact time I picked up

Solutions chapter and I haven't yet finished it. Disgusting? Yeah.

I've also noticed that these days I didn't have any breaks scheduled and when it was scheduled I intentionally took even bigger breaks. Interesting, right? How did this foolish ass decision exist in the first place? Well, I had a breakdown because I wasted time and then when I made the strategy I was freaking out and was running out of time so I decided to cut out two hours from the dinner and lunch and study extra or I could just say I tried to compensate which I know is even worse.

I am tired a lot like a lot just because I've been hard working all my life and I could have had worked smartly like many people do manage their boards and entrance exam as well. Well, it's not always about entrance exams, I'm just saying that they manage multiple things. Had I known that I'd never be able to get past 94% in any of my board exams I'd

have had not done more than 94% I don't know the reason why I'm saying this right now but my health is so degraded and all studies have bought me all my life is first rank in school that no one really cares about and a whole bunch of ailments.

I do not know how to work under stressful situations, like I prepared for my tenth exam for at least three months on the go I know it's very unusual because no one needs that much amount of time but I did eight revisions during that time man! I'm addicted to revisions and when I don't do them I just fail, my hands are hurting right now, my head is too.

Over the course of coming days, my health got worse, I couldn't look at anything in order to study, my stomach was relieved from not having coffee anymore, but my eye pain and headache was getting worse, and we had to book an urgent appointment to an eye clinic. I visited there with my mom, I hadn't been out of my house for over a month, so we took a detour and did some brisk shopping on the way. The doctor told me that I had strained my eyes, and gave me a bunch of eye drops, and I also got myself an anti-blue ray glass, but to be honest it was just a treat.

Chapter Nine

June 23rd, 2022. Four days to go

One of the things that the ophthalmologist had told me was to avoid screen time, which I couldn't do completely but I still followed the instructions- while at my core I was just procrastinating. I knew that I wouldn't be able to revise physics, so, I had given up on that, and the only thing left was chemistry. I had also made a point to talk to my mom and Convey her of the fact that my preparation was in ruins, I told her that it was because I'd been sick for over a week that I couldn't revise anything – which wasn't a lie. She was mortified to hear that, because all I had done in my life was to prepare for exams and then slay them, this was different, she started behaving frantically, but she didn't protest much after seeing the way I was quivering, and what she asked was a very fundamental question that I didn't know the answer to, couldn't know, she said, "You've been preparing for this exam for so long, or were you just bluffing and pretending that you were?" I replied by saying that no, I had been preparing only, and it was because I had not been able to revise since past few days that I was doomed. She kept looking at me, thinking that I was lying, and she said, "But what about all the preparation that you did, you don't remember that you ever studied?"

"It always happens, no matter how much I prepare, I have to do everything all over again, around five days before exam, or otherwise I forget everything. It's always been like that," and that was the most sincere answer that I could give to her, and somehow she believed it but only after I told her that exactly one month after this exam, another JEE test would be conducted, and this one would become insignificant if I happen to get less marks. After hearing that, she began to emphasize and console me by saying that, "Don't panic, it's all going to be alright," I wonder why she didn't say the same thing before I told her that there was a way out.

June 24th, 2022. Three days to go.

By this time, I'd already realised that I didn't have a chance in the first session of tests, but I still had to take the test anyway because my mom told me, so obviously I shouldn't have been slouching or scrolling the YouTube, but I was. Once again my eyes had start to hurt while watching the videos on news related to the notification of admit cards and I had landed on a channel that made videos on various multi-billion dollar companies and how they came to be. They all had fascinating stories, and humble backgrounds and watching all that struggle and hardships all of them had to go through was inspiring, but what wasn't inspiring was to hear the ticking of clock in the pouring rain and pain in my eyes which was only escalated by being on my phone. By ditching physics, I had had this fake sense of relief that now I have enough time to study and all I have to do was revise chemistry which I had done so many times that it wasn't going to take any long, and I thought that watching YouTube for a little bit wouldn't hurt, but it was almost twelve O' clock and all I had done was to Panic because of the admit card notification news as everything seemed to get real and concrete with that, and watch random YouTube videos. I knew I had to do something about it, but before taking any real steps to do something about it, I Stumbled on another video.

I knew what I was doing was wrong, and I had to stop but I Just couldn't, so I thought I lacked motivation and I plugged my earphones and started playing the 'Fight song' thinking that It might get me in the form of working, which it didn't, the lyrics, "but I've still got a lot of fight left in me," felt pointless because I didn't have anything in me to fight with. I started playing "stand by you" but I didn't cry this time after hearing the lyrics "I'll walk through hell with you, love you're not alone, I'm gonna stand by you," but what I did feel was sense of disgust that how could I stand by myself, what would standing by myself mean if I failed? I would become a failure if I would fail, and there was no point in feeling bad about it, or better yet, trying to do anything about it. Basically there was no point in trying to be compassionate towards myself. I tuned into "who says," but there was no point in hearing, "Who says you don't past the test," because nobody had told me that I couldn't, everybody would just say, "You're gifted but you're not living up to your full potential, just try a bit harder," which had made me believe it, but it was just me now thinking that I couldn't pass the test. There was nobody that I would envision while listening to the lyrics, "the earth can pull you down with all its gravity," and I felt disgusted by hearing, "and the measure of your worth is sometimes hard to see," because it wasn't, the measure of my worth was the exam that I was going to take and ultimately fail. The only lyrics that almost started a spark in me were:

"When the fire is at my feet again, when the vultures all start circling, don't be surprised but still I'll rise," it was the only song that didn't include any sense of nonsense compassion towards myself, but supported the narrative of getting up and trying again. And just when I lifted the pen in my hands and adjusted my posture by sitting up, I got a call from my dad saying that the lunch was served.

I went into my room thinking that now I would study only to realise that I couldn't. The fact that all the songs that I had heard didn't have any effect on me made me think that I was chasing the wrong horse, or fish, momentarily because I got hit with the realisation that I had messed up the numbers – the number of hours, the number of hours left- because apparently the number of hours you study determines how smart shaped your ass is. I'd assigned less time to every chapter so I started panicking and out of that panicking got my ass back up and kicking. But what I realised as I started revising was that even after doing all the spaced repetitions that I had done, I still couldn't remmember things clearly, or to my satisfaction. For the first time I started questioning my abilities because how was it even possible that you wouldn't be able to reproduce anything at all when you have done it for well over ten times, was something wrong with me? Anyhow, I started with organic chemistry, luckily I had made micro notes and I revised them. It took two days to complete doing so.

June 26th, 2022. One day to go.

My day started in the state of panic, but I subsided that feeling and decided to use whatever time I'd left of the daylight judiciously. I had to go see a doctor because my blood pressure had gone up and I spent the entire morning freaking out and being hysterical. And while having lunch a panic attack, this time it had manifested in a physical form too, my hands begin to shake and I spilled the water all over my food from the glass which was in my hands as I tried to drink it, my stomach felt like it was in knots and that I could throw up, my mom panicked seeing this, but I made a point to not look her in order to not get any sympathy because it had felt fake the last time after realising it. My dad didn't even realise anything was wrong at all, I didn't even think about it because I knew it was pointless. I tried using a timer because in the middle of all this, I still somehow found reasons to wander mentally, I surfed from one chapter to the other, rambling on and everything seemed foreign, once again. I tried using my verbal learning techniques but it was useless, and just like that it was five in the evening. I had given up, completely and could totally see my doom. On one hand, it didn't matter because I had one more chance but then on the another side it mattered a lot, I had spent a great deal of my life preparing for it and my perfectionist ego was getting hurt. I went downstairs in an attempt to totally dissociate myself from all the load and get a breath of fresh air, I had my evening tea and snacks with my parents and it helped. We drew out a plan that I was going to be packing my stuff first thing after taking the test. I first time in well over a month slept on time for I had to wake up on time too.

June 27th, 2022. THE D DAY.

I woke up, took a bath, had a light breakfast and attempted to revise my posted notes and failed because I had forgotten them too. We booked a cab to reach the exam centre as it was located in the outskirts of the town and on my way there all I did was panic and attempt to revise the formulas in physics from my dad's phone only to realize I'd forgotten that as well. The whole time we had to wait for the gates to open while everybody else was talking to their friends all I did was to be on my phone it was the first too, before this day I had never been the guy with their eyes glued to the notebook an hour before exam at examination hall, but here I was feeling cryptic in my skin and as if my bones had been stoned with the nails, and all my nerves too and all I could feel was pain. The cool breeze that was blowing, my father trying to talk to me and all the chatter got lost in the background, and the only thing I could hear was the rhythm of my heart which was beating at a diabolically insane pace. I knew about all the psychological tricks that tell you to not revise hurriedly before an important exam but I still did it in an attempt to get a sense of not giving up or maybe from an underlying feeling of fear.

We went through a lot of security checks before they let us take our designated seats. We waited for everybody to get seated and then the question paper flashed on our computer screens.

Physics was the first subject, but from whatever wisdom I had, I chose to go for my strongest subject; Chemistry. I read the first question and it wasn't that difficult. I powered through first four questions and then there was a question from the organic section based on the topic that I didn't know but from the chapter that Anirudh had taught us, and then the another one, and then the third one. It had started to register in my mind that he had not taught us those topics but I didn't do anything about it except take a sip of water. And then worse the chapters that I had not done and from what I learned from the stats, only three to four questions from those chapters had been asked in past years at tops, but my paper was flooded with those questions from those chapters which made me lose my mind. Having a knowhow, a basic knowledge of stats is good but the educators on YouTube make you practice a certain set of questions from past year papers and publicly claim those are the questions that you're going to get asked, and then they guarantee you. Actually, they teach you a topic based around a particular set of questions and then make you do those questions, it makes you think they taught us what comes in the exam. Now I don't know about anybody else but I was desperate and running out of time- which nobody seemed to understand not even Heidi; people would think that I was trying to play a victim card when I'd said there are people who prepare for this exam for years and I just got half a year which was the absolute truth – so, I believed it superficially because I knew if I'd start listening to what my critical part of brain would say I'd regret not preparing for the exam. So there I was in the exam hall cussing out all those educators as their evil grins after seeing what they were doing to the students, making a mock in the name of mock tests would flash across my brain.

So far it was not that bad, but it got bad when I saw the physical section of chemistry- the typical numerical sum type problems- I read the first question and it was easy, I attempted to do it and after understanding the concept of the questions all I had to do was put in the given data in an equation but there was no equation, as in, the formula that would lead me to that equation had wiped out of my brain. It caused a great deal of stress but I sucked it up and I thought maybe I'd be able to recall it later. I jumped to the next question and the same thing happened. I knew the question, I was able to understand them but I couldn't recall those stupid formulas.

Escalated with all the chattering in the exam hall that would make me look up from my cubicle to everywhere and the bird peeing near my desktop, the pain of frustration turned into a full blown frustration. If it wasn't for the time limit I'd have jumped out of the window from the panic attack. I didn't know what to do, I was going to fail the exam, and everybody who had told me that they had high expectations from me kept booing into my ears and I ultimately had to shut down.

I took a breath for ten minutes and imagined the worst possible scenario which kind of helped, as it also reminded me of the fact that this was not the end of the world. I had moved on, metaphorically and literally from chemistry onto the physics section. I had already planned to leave physics, but I attempted to read some anyway. Starting out were the questions from the chapters that I hadn't done or the ones that I had done but were difficult so there was no point even attempting them, because if all of this isn't enough, the exam criteria is coupled with the negative marking so you don't attempt a certain question just because you feel like it. And then there were some questions that I actually was able to solve but I had this weird thing of using a random formula that would be related to the context rather than the simple one. Mr. Maher would call it "gripping your ear from behind your head behaviour." It was one of those things that I didn't know why I did, but ultimately it wasted time. Cool thing that I only had to do physics and chemistry at most so it was not that big of a problem.

Sharon writes something down and says, "Yeah not a problem because you had all the time in the galaxy, but what about the overwhelm and the fuss that would come with it, did you ever take that into consideration?"

"Hey, don't blast me, okay! I never quite understood it" I throw my hands in the air.

The time was up. As we emerged out of the building through the front gate, I saw my dad waiting for me there and as always he was expecting me to tell him that I'd given a 'breathtakingly beautiful test,' which I hadn't. I had planned to remain stoic and have no expression on my face. He asked and I gave him a dead answer, we walked for ten minutes and then my uncle picked us up. I don't know if he hadn't said it how I'd have been on the drive home, but he consoled me by saying that it was all OK and there was nothing to worry about, rare thing in our family.

I have this thing of losing perspectives, and him telling me that it wasn't a big deal helped me gain my perspective back that I still have one more shot left and things would get better. He dropped us halfway and we walked home. I knew, even after conveying to her prior, my mom would throw a tantrum when I tell her that my exam was bad, so I tried reverse psychology by throwing a tantrum myself, which worked. The only human being that seemed to see anything positive with all of this was Heidi. She seemed exhilarated because she had known every day the ordeal I would put myself through but even after all that I had not given up, and she kept telling me that it was because I had been sick that all of this had happened and also that it was now in my hands to make it better. She advised me to take a day off which I did. As planned that I would pack all my stuff – well half of it because I still had to study so some of it still needed to be kept – and then we had dinner but before sleeping, I received a call from my cousin – Kareem and his wife Irtiqa. As always Kareem asked me how it went and now his wife too and I said what my honest truth was. On a normal day, I get a more than 95% result and Kareem acts like he isn't satisfied- I suppose that has got to do with him being the oldest child- but this time he didn't say anything, and Irtiqa told me that it was OK and that I had to put my health first, and that I was going to rock next time because, and I quote "You're a Topper." What was aimed to make me feel better, also ended up giving me insane amount of anxiety in a weird way, I hated that all people did was to expect highly of me, I was genuinely tired of this Topper persona, which was slipping from my hands anyways. By this time it had started to feel like a Jail, because no matter which way I'd go it would catch up to me, and there wasn't many directions to go either.

I ended the call and started my Ted talk – where I was a speaker obviously- I spoke about all the mistakes that I had done and how I could solve them and counter the mess that I created to my audience that comprised of my closet and my bed, and I had to cut it short when I realized that there wasn't physically anybody else in the room, and go to sleep.

I woke up in a good season; having the knowledge on burn outs and the importance of taking a break. It was planned I was going to take a break, only I didn't take one. I was completely charged with enthusiasm and ready to give this exam my best shot after the break would be over, but picking up my phone seemed more exciting at the moment as it was one of those things that I had to let go of in order to be extra disciplined- extra because for me it's always been extreme case scenario; there rarely was a middle ground; I'd either have to abandon doing something, or I'd only be doing that thing even if it would kill me from the inside- and I started scrolling YouTube because that's the only social media platform that I couldn't delete from my phone and because of this I had my breakfast late than usual, and that's how pretty much that day went, I wanted to take a break but all I did was do things without planning which didn't give me any sense of break, it felt like my life was on autopilot and I was stuck and directionless. I was lousy and Slouchy but most of the time I was in my head, I was thinking of that home design that I had been thinking about the night before as well, I pictured different intricacies of it; how the kitchen would look like, how was dining going to be, how my room would look like, to the point that I couldn't make myself not think about it, whatever I did it was playing at the back of my head, and by the end of the day my head was heavy like it had been tied to an anchor and I was exhausted from all the brainstorming, and all I had done that day was to be in my head, spend time without any regard, and attempt to make a couple of logos for my future business which I may or may not have scrapped because I ended up hating the way all of them looked, hence I didn't take any rest, but I tried convincing myself that tomorrow was going to be different, that I would stop day dreaming and get serious about my studies.

I woke up the next day, and grabbed my phone to set the tone for the coming day (to be lousy). The same thing happened, I delayed my meals because of being late, and all I could think about was that architectural plan that I had been imagining, but it didn't stop there, I started thinking of all the businesses I was going to do one day, and one thing that I had realised by now was that I don't remember what I had been thinking even hours after, let alone ten or twelve years in future- I was aware that thinking about anything was futile. Backed up by manifestation, and dream board stuff everybody on internet was talking about, I made sure to write every dream collaboration I could think of, and just like that I was swept into the world where nobody had the audacity to interfere me, and all my emotions and dreams were respected, and I had the free will to do everything, and to be everything, the world of dreams, or should I say day dreams.

Another thing that I had learned by this time was the fact that dreaming isn't actually bad, and all those great people that have walked this planet and would talk about dreaming weren't wrong, dreaming was actually good, it's the only hope, only sliver of hope one can cling to, in order to get into their higher form of self, it's what makes life exciting and worth living. Now I wouldn't be me, if I wouldn't talk about dreams in regard to working class because that's also an aspect I have to introspect about, and three years into the concept of entrance test, and JEE, YouTube algorithm started showing me all these videos of people who hadn't taken the conventional path in order to succeed, were kicking ass, and the substitutes to the colleges and universities that we the aspirants of JEE were supposed to be joining weren't pieces of shit- they also mattered, and had a valuable place in the world. So, I didn't stop dreaming, I dreamed all I could, for the first time in a long time, and it made me feel that the only end of the world is the end of the world itself, nothing else is; that sky isn't the limit; that there is a world to be reached and a surface to be touched even beyond sky, and the only thing that awaited me was to give myself permission to be open and let my imagination go wild and dream about having the world because in that moment I felt like I deserved it, I deserved every great experience in this world. I would have continued, but my dad called on my cell because my mom had served the lunch.

I ran upstairs after we had lunch, so that I could get that home design that was bothering me on paper. I started playing All too well TV (10 mins version), because Taylor's storytelling had started to feel more compelling as the days passed by since I first started thinking of getting my thoughts on paper, and I started drawing that design, and while I was at it, my brain kept thinking of the ways, of the exact time I was going to get that house; it was either I would get the house at the most perfect time in the world or I'd be living in rags- that's exactly what my demons told me, like I said I live on extremes. It took me well over three hours to get it done and it looked beautiful, so I had to send it to Heidi, and I could feel her gasping as she sent me the series of text messages as an indication. I convinced myself that I was saving myself the money that it'd take me to get an architect to design a home plan for me. I was done with drawing that home design but the chain of thoughts just made me stuck, I could feel the bedsheet beneath me feel as if it wasn't there, my legs started to get numb and my eye sockets started to hurt as I kept thinking but I didn't move, I tried to, several times but every time I'd start to think of a different facet of some vague architecture. And by the time I was over it, it was almost dinner time as the Maghrib Calls started to emerge from across the street, and I had to get up to draw the blinds and turn on the lights.

After the dinner was over, I started to make a plan for the next session of JEE test only to end up getting overwhelmed with all the stuff that I had to numb myself to sleep before my brain would start making me think things. I spend the next two days in what I later came to realise as 'Analysis paralysis' because all these YouTubers we're talking about how small the duration of time between two events was, and that we deserved more time in between, they'd also tell you to not lend your ears onto people that'd tell you that exam was getting delayed but that's exactly what you do. You try to tell and convince yourself that you're not going to listen to rumours that tell you that there's an easy way to life only to realise that you end up getting sucked in that hellhole with each passing second, but the key point is that *when you are a damsel in distress- regardless of gender.* I texted Heidi and we decided on what we we're going to do in the coming days.

"Pardon me, but, Ahmad, why would you have to text Heidi about all of this? Was she in the same field as yours," Sharon stops me to ask me, and I answer by saying,

"Well, no, she wasn't in the same field per se but you know she was my friend, she had been there for me for the most part," I tell her but it's clear that I don't really mean that to be the reason.

"So?"

"Honestly? I wanted somebody to tell me that what I was doing was right, I needed somebody to validate me," I scoff and tell her.

"What I believe is that it came from a place of thinking that you weren't capable of making a decision and that you needed somebody's assistance on doing that," she adds, but I already know, I had to know that long ago in order to be something in my life, after that therapy session in 2023.

THE BREAKING POINT

Chapter ten.

ONE LAST TIME. July 1st, 2022.

Perfectionism has been one of the biggest enemies of mine throughout my life, I used to have this fantasy that there was going to be a perfect day, a perfect week where I would do everything on my schedule perfectly down to its last detail, and if that wouldn't be, then I'd rather waste an entire day.

The similar thing happened, although it was accompanied with disgust as well, when I finally thought of studying again for I had wasted four days, I was doomed and the schedule was doomed as well, and I already felt like I had less time and that I wouldn't be able to make it.

In retrospection, in my defence this happened because I had no control or regard over my thoughts, they'd turn wild anytime, and what I needed was a little bit of introspection that I didn't have to complete every single thing, and also that four days didn't mean a lot when I had twenty six days left, also that out of those four days; two had been for taking rest, that's the problem with me- my brain will remind me of all the bad memories like I said earlier to further catastrophize the situation, it got so bad that I was scared to even start. And it was also a deeply rooted excuse to not do physics *numericals* in particular.

But then after spending a day like this, I had to start so I attempted to do it only I wasn't able to regulate my focus, my thoughts would go wild, I might or might not think anything in particular but I wouldn't be able to regulate my focus. Was it because I was terrified of doing *numericals* and the way my mind and body would react to it, or because I was so obsessed with starting other venues that I'd been thinking about and all these different architectural designs? I didn't understand. But what I did know was that the clock was ticking and whatever I was doing needed to stop, I needed to be resilient, because I couldn't let all the hard work that I had supposedly done to go into ruins, and then one afternoon while I was taking a bath- something I normally wouldn't do but did that day as a way to procrastinate- I had soap all over my hands and from all the conflict that I was in, I picked up a razor in order to shave not realising that It could slip from my hands and injure me, and the next thing you know is that it did. While I was shaving it slipped from my hand, and before it would touch any vital organ of my body, I was quick to grip it with the hands that had soap on but it slipped in a way that as it fell down to the ground it took a flesh of my pinkie with it and before I could process what had happened, the bathroom floor was covered with the red blood, and it was my right hand. I tried running my hand under water in order to stop the bleeding but it wasn't just a cut, it felt like half of my pinkie had been cut off. While I Still had the soap all over my body, I tried gripping a bathroom towel around my finger and my hand so that I could wash the soap off of my body and come out of the bathroom. I struggled to put on a pair of shorts and my T shirt with a hand that was now a bulge with the towel covering it and I emerged out of the bathroom and rushed to the kitchen so that my mom could wear a proper bandage around it. I knew this would come up as she started getting angry at why I had injured myself, like it had been my conscious decision to hurt myself, and I had let my parents scold me every time I had been sick, and make me feel bad, and from all that was happening I had developed mental strength to tell her to shut up because I wasn't liking the sensation of blood dripping from my finger at the rate it was dripping, and forcing its way out through the bandage as my knees were turning wobbly at the same time listening to the senseless yelling as to why I hurt myself.

The significance of this incident is evident; my brain was completely zoning out all the time- because of all that hysteria I don't remember but maybe I was thinking of the same home designs in the bathroom as well- and I was becoming UNHINGED with every passing day, and now it was a challenge to study because physics *numericals* require you to use your hand, one could still be able to study even after this, but my brain starts to shut down during inconveniences and needless to say my life was upside down.

I spend the day traumatised because what I had done in the bathroom by not panicking was brave- at least it was to me- but I still hadn't recovered from the impact of it, and then we went to the construction site, it was exciting to see that my home was getting build, part by part, one brick at a time, *only if the excitement had lasted!*

Over the next few days what ensued were regular visits to the construction site, as from of escapism, and because the neighbours were being tough on the workers. But it was paired with a lot of frustration as I wouldn't be able to write down anything, I don't exactly remember where that motivation had come from but I had wanted to "cut the crap and just do the *numericals*" but I couldn't write anything so it was futile, as my obsessions with day dreaming and architecture escalated; I used to draw different home designs while my mom would feed me because with bandages covering my hand I couldn't even lift anything with my own hands, not even a spoon to feed myself. As the days passed by the same question of "Why am I doing this?" started to rake up from within me as I realised that this truly wasn't the only way to succeed in life as I'd also seen on YouTube. I wouldn't remember even a single thing if I ever would sit down to study, and solve a numerical. I had accepted the fact that my memory was totally flawed by this time but hell, I still expected to reproduce something, anything, after all these months of studying and preparation, at least something, while I was annoyed by my lack of being able to do anything at the same time I was constantly feeling guilty, I was guilty that I was hating the subjects that I once used to love. I hated the fact that I wasn't able to concentrate, I hated that I wasn't focusing on things that mattered, and I had chosen but had no problem in thinking about interior designs, business plans and book ideas all day long.

"In hindsight, I wish I hadn't done that, you know apart from everything that was happening, I didn't need to feel guilty for that as well, it was the last thing that should have happened." I say as I regret and mourn for the boy that I was in 2022.

"What thing?"

"You know feeling guilty that I had fallen out of love with my core subjects- which by the way wasn't the case," I answer.

Heightened by the disgust, being annoyed and anger I started researching on how I could become successful by taking other paths. I also made a business plan that I was going to execute, and the only thing I needed was to get the money that I would start with. The journal entry that I had started a few months ago – Which I ultimately had stopped when nothing seemed to work – had turned into a full on book idea, I thought I was going to call it "Through My Eyes," and it was going to be a book about a guy who spends his life being misunderstood and clearing those misunderstandings and making the whole thing awkward during the process. I was day dreaming now, I thought my book was going to be a bestseller and that it would help me kick-start my business, and I had nothing to worry about.

I woke up next morning and whatever I had planned to do last night made and had made me excited was cut short when I began to think about the money that I didn't have to start with. Whatever I had dreamt about yesterday felt like a fantasy, it felt unachievable, and once again, here I was with another lost perspective of the belief that your dreams need to look like a fantasy so that when you fulfil them you live the life of fantasy. And I needed to have something promising, something that would promise me results, because now it wasn't just the JEE, it was to start the chain reaction; the chain reaction to where my life would begin again, but I Just needed a Little spark and I wanted to make sure I have enough spark to begin with, and once again, and because it was true as well, if you'd do JEE you'd get that head start. After having my breakfast, I first time in a long time opened a notebook and attempted to write something and when I couldn't I knew I needed to have a deeper conversation with myself, I knew I needed to connect with my soul.

Journal entry July 8th, 2022:

"This is impossible now. I know words have impact, but this is, and I think I'm not going to make it- although I didn't want to say that- but yeah whatever, let's just not *say* it. But whatever happens, I promise that I'm going to stick with myself till the end, no matter what happens, I need to take care of myself. This is not the end of the world. I know everything is about to turn into a joke, and I'm going to regret the fact that I am the only reason responsible for having wasted all the efforts that I put into it; all the all-nighters, but I am not going to let any of that affect me to think differently. My health matters, my mental health matters, and no matter what anybody says, at the end of it I'm going to make it out alive, that's what matters, I'm alive, I am going to be full of life, I'm going to make it through the other end of it. I matter. I know what I think right now might feel like the easy way to go about the situation; because it's not only failing; it's failing even after being so close, almost getting the feel of it like one feels the rays of sunshine sift on their face through the window, but I can't be like everyone else. I need to RISE, I need to FIGHT BACK, I need to STAND BY MYSELF, I can't think of it- I can't, I won't- I am not going to end my life, I'm not attempting suicide even if I might feel like a burden and unlovable but I know that's not the best way. I Just know it.

Musaib Bilal, I'm sorry. Please forgive me. I thank you. I love you. And I promise you that I'm going to take care of you, and whatever happens is going to be ultimately in your favour, I just have faith in almighty.

"That reference that everything was going to be great ultimately and in my favour. That was delusional. You know why? Because even at that moment I was at the conflict that, maybe I will take the test one

more time, or maybe something else happens, like I'd always thought it would."

"I know I know it sounds ridiculous me going back to it again but that's the point, my mind had been made so occupied with the thought of it that wherever I looked in order to succeed I sought it," I stop to tell her.

"Don't say that, it's not ridiculous, nothing is ever ridiculous about a human being, and we may not understand something from the limited knowledge that we all possess but that doesn't make anything ridiculous. And like you said, it wasn't your fault but it was the continuous repetition that coded it into your subconscious mind, that's why you only sought it for wherever, or whenever you looked for other streams to succeed," she adds to my list of revelation and one more muscle in my brain relaxes and eases out after being open like a window for all these years.

After completing that journal entry, I made one more plan, yes again, but this time I did it so that I could feel a sense of resilience in me- that feeling of not giving up- even if I knew I wasn't going to follow through the plan. And yet again, the plan included me sacrificing the Eid holidays.

I woke up on the day of Eid at 7 am, usually it would be at around three in the morning, as planned because I wanted no part in the celebrations; all I wanted was to study, although it hurt me even to think that that's how I was going to spend the coming days. I didn't wish anybody, I didn't post any story on my socials, I didn't do anything, in fact, I posted a story telling my family, friends and relatives that if they we're interested they could wish me a happy Eid because I had made my mind that I wasn't going to. I didn't work; I didn't study that day rather I spent the morning mourning that I had to, and that I wasn't. I ultimately gave up when I called everybody and greeted them because nobody cared. I knew I wasn't going to be doing any studies, not on the day of Eid. I might not have studied but that didn't mean I didn't deserve to take a break, because my mind had been active and working extra hours all that time too, it also deserved a break. I had promised that I was going to let myself be happy without any second thought, while I tried not to think about the plan that I had sketched. I spend the Eid like I would, had fun, even so that I stretched the three day break to five day break, it would've lasted longer but my mom begin to get sceptical so I had to mask till I was ready to tell her the truth.

On the sixth day of Eid, I picked up my books and I walked myself through the torment of knowing that I had let it slip through my hands like sand, but something in me just wasn't ready to blame me. Maybe it was that journal entry but whatever it was, I felt a tight knot in my stomach.

"What I didn't tell you is that I had spent all this time numbing myself in the name of not giving up, I had felt the feelings of depression and because I had thought what I had taken for depression in 2020 had been stupid, I had told myself that I wasn't

depressed, I would actively tell myself that you are not depressed, you can't be depressed," I say.

"Looking back at it now, it breaks my heart because it's as if I look in the mirror, I see my younger self or maybe it's my own child, and I tell them, and I dictate to them the way they should feel. I'm almost ashamed that I did that being the one who wanted to spread the word of importance of mental health, I did that to myself," I add, "excuse me," when I sniffle.

"You can't do that to yourself. You can't blame yourself for all of it. Although I can see that boy getting hurt but you can't walk around carrying the weight of all of it on your shoulders. I don't want to dismiss the way you feel towards your younger self, but know that you made it, you're here, and you look back to the guy you were and you feel deeply sorry for him, that's enough suffering for you to go through," she sighs.

"I then out of nowhere began typing "Depression" in the search engine, but what I also did was I added the keywords

like "unable to focus," "overthinking," "zoning out," in a desperate attempt to find a magic pill and what I saw would change the way I looked at my life forever."

"Good god!" Sharon exclaims which feels like she actually intended to say, "Holy shit," as a smirk plays across her face.

And what I saw was a wide range of symptoms that I'd been showing for, hell most part of my life but had been prevalent that year. I came across a name of a condition called,

"ADHD," I can hear Sharon visibly gasp as she shifts in her chair, "This changes everything, about and about the dynamic with your dad."

"Yup"

"So you knew it all along? What did you do after that?"

"I wanted to do something right away but that didn't happen, it was a little complicated than that but all the guilt that I had felt was gone, it faded into thin air and the next thing I did was to text Heidi."

"It seems like she's been a significant part of your journey, isn't it? What did you tell her and how did she react to it?" She asks.

"In hindsight I don't even know how I would have wanted her to react; react to the news that your friend supposedly suffers from a neurological condition. Because whenever we talk of ADHD, or that article that I sent her, it kept coming back to how good you were in studies, and the fact that I had never gotten less than 95% in my school and she knew it, but she also knew that I hated the exam, I don't know, if I was her, maybe I would've thought that I'm using it as an excuse, otherwise it would've been all along, present," I tell her.

"She told me that she would never give up on me. "I'd never give up on you, but I don't know how to help you, the only person that can help you now is a therapist,""

"Although I wanted her to acknowledge it more than she did, but she suggested me that I should go to a therapist," I add.

"The only thing that is in your hands right now is to do the revision," she texted to

which I replied by saying, "Just forget it," and then I didn't text her for two days.

"I told her to forget it because in my hearts of hearts I knew that It was over, everything was over, I was only doing it as a way to not give up just like promised," I tell her.

"I'm glad that she suggested you to go to a therapy, but did you join it?" She asks.

"Well that's got to be one of the reasons why I stand here because what ensued after the second attempt tore me apart. But it eventually felt like it was the LAST SUMMER THAT I LIVED that pathetic life," I tell her.

"Oh yeah?" She seems taken away by what I said, and she adds, "Seems like we're up to a happy ending after all."

"That depends on when you decide a specific story ends," I tell her as I pucker my brow with a grin on my face.

Chapter Eleven.

One week to go.

"What the bug are you talking about?" My mom shouted when I told her about what had been going on for a month because the condition was worse, I would feel paralysed by now; I'd open my books and just before I'd know my mind had been drifted and I'd be stuck till the hours had gone by, it was summer and I wore shorts and the fan would be on, I could feel the cool air from the fan hit my legs and the pain that would rise within my legs, but it was as if there was a magnet that'd keep me stuck to the ground, and I couldn't get up.

I thought she'd be supportive of me when I told her that it was impossible to make because I had this belief that although my parents are strict, they are not that strict, but when I told my mom about this she started getting angry and accused me of things like Scrolling internet, having a girlfriend, spending my nights on my phone. I looked into her eyes and I felt this twist in my stomach because I felt like a product, a brand at that moment; a machine that you discard once it starts breaking down.

"What are the relatives going to say? They'll think that you've indulged in drugs or other love-stuff. What am I going to tell them when they ask me what do you keep doing in that room of yours? I don't understand anything at all. The main question is what do you actually keep doing in there with the lock on?" She burst out on me.

I didn't have an answer about the locking the door from the inside because the ritual had started because of them coming into my room which would make me lose the focus. Similarly like that year too, I'd enter my room thinking to study but lately the overthinking would take over. But what I also realised was that she was throwing all the jabs at me and using the relatives as an Alias. She added one humiliation to another and I kept silent because I didn't have an answer, but one thing I knew and remember was the promise that I made to myself and seeing her behave that way only helped me see clearly who truly was by my side for me, and not just for any material gains, I knew I was completely alone.

"Do one thing now. Don't go into that cramped hole of yours," she referenced to my room, "and spend the rest of the time here so that if anybody asks I'll tell them that you were here by my side, helping me with packing or anything related to moving," she continued.

"You see this thing of me loosing Perspective and forgetting things, I forgot to tell her that I'd made them to tell everybody that I'd take admission next year so that if anything goes wrong, I could bounce back from it without the burden for having to think about what people would say," I tell Sharon.

"What did we spend all this money for? For nothing," she added as I let myself be consumed with guilt. And after getting all the frustration out that had been pent up from the family feud, she asked me, "What do you actually keep doing in there?" And for the first time I replied by saying, "I just think, and I cannot control it," and then I tried to remind her of the time in 2020 when I'd told her that I might have depression and that I needed to see a psychiatrist, which she denied by saying, "No, I don't remember any of that," but I didn't budge and when she accepted that she remembered, she said, "Yes, I remember and just like I told you back then, what is everybody going to think of it? Because I might not tell anyone, but your father will go on telling everybody, just this month on Eid your dad told everybody that you took the test and failed it," she said.

I replied by saying, "We shouldn't care about what anybody says, and why is it that if someone has a cold, they get to see a doctor without any second thoughts, but if somebody's brain has caught a cold, they can't go to see a therapist?"

"There is someone else I know who was also eccentric before marriage, he'd throw things around, he even once almost assaulted me and your father with a knife, but nobody even thought of taking him to see a doctor, so that we don't deem him UNHINGED," she told me.

"Well, that's the problem, because he didn't get to join therapy, he'll only ever be like that, and also the fact that it's not necessary everybody who has some difficulty with their brain, they're all unhinged, we need to let go of this notion, and move past this stigma," I replied.

"I also made a point to tell her that I was not a machine, and that even a machine breaks down but she didn't care about that. She basically wanted me to supress all my mental health struggles. I also told her that it takes one or two years to prepare for this exam, and even after that some people don't crack it. To which she replied by saying that I had made my mind and there was nothing that could be done," I tell Sharon.

I add, "I didn't know how to respond to that because all of what was happening, it was out of my control, and I had busted my ass for four months so that I don't have to wait for years, and there she was accusing me of it when I needed her to be a shoulder I could cry on, I hated the way I used to look into her eyes and love her more than I'd loved god."

"She also told me that I should pray more often because I didn't have to do anything else. I didn't have any problem with praying, in fact it was one of those things that my heart would cry for because it had become less and less in quantity over the years, but the problem was that I wasn't in control of my executive functioning anymore, but she wouldn't understand that."

"But, you wouldn't know this, this was the story of 99% of brown families back then, while our parents were growing up nobody had emphasized with them because one way or other everyone was a product of some kind of major trauma, and everybody's first priority was survival. Folks from my generation, we grew up in peculiar times, the time of modernization while at the same time there were still some people fighting for their survival, and didn't know what

they would eat and feed their children in the evening, if they would. Sometimes it wouldn't feel fair to compare our traumas with people who were homeless and were making it through the life one day at a time. Although that doesn't mean that I wouldn't feel that my parents were being extra traumatising," I say in one breath.

"Okay first of all, ALL TRAUMA IS VALID," she speaks it to my face word by word. She goes on saying, "Imagine someone who plays rugby regularly, and someone who doesn't, both get hurt, doubtlessly the one who doesn't play rugby will get more hurt, because their body hasn't known that level of trauma, while at the same time the rugby guy won't feel anything at all. And nevertheless, it doesn't matter what kind of trauma any of us goes through, the basic human feelings and emotions aren't special to just one person, your brain feels the same pain when you get into a physical fight and when the love of your life breaks up with you."

THE ROAD TO SELF REDEMPTION

Chapter twelve

Exam day. Session two. July 27th, 2022.

I wake up in a good season, take a bath and have breakfast, the same cab driver as last time picked me up, alone this time; my dad was home and so was his phone. Unlike last time, I didn't spend the commute time being stuck with my notes, I was present in the moment, I took in everything. And when we reached there, I wasn't as pathetic as the last time, I knew It was very difficult to make it, but for last few days I had started to think deeply about it, and started to accept the reality that whatever was coming my way would be in my favour, and a little bit of faith on all the revisions that I had done. I had to wait for an hour before they let us in the exam hall, and I made a little chat with the people sitting right next to me which made me feel good, I was at peace, the journal entry had helped, it didn't take much to be happy while at the same time accept the reality.

Just like the last time, I started with chemistry, only this time I was at peace and could see through the difficult and non-difficult questions, I did the easy ones in one go, and focused on the difficult ones after them, but before I could breakdown like I did last time, I made a point to stop and breathe. I breathed in, breathed out for a few minutes as I looked at the flower meadows through the window very far away on a sunny day, and when I felt ready, I started again. I left all the questions that needed me to remember the formulas and equations, and I turned to the physics section and I was able to do some ten odd questions, which made twenty five questions in total and if all of them would be correct I could get easily get an admission in a local NIT, in a not so fascinating branch of engineering but basically I could at least "qualify the test".

I emerged from the exam hall and I had made my mind that I wasn't going to be pathetic which would make everybody else pathetic too, but also because I had done twenty five question that had given me a new hope, so after seeing my dad I smiled lightly and when he asked, I told him that It was nice, not disclosing much, he asked me was it great, I only said it was good, and we headed home.

My mom was happy to hear that I'd done better than the last time, while I didn't know if all the questions that I had answered were correct or not, but there still was a chance

I next texted Heidi.

"Broooo

It went well than the last time duhh

I was talking to Gagan. She will send me the details of a mental health professional

I did twenty three questions, last time seventeen only

I can get into metallurgy majors here at NIT

But I don't think I'll be joining that.

But at the same time thinking that I might have to do it for one more year could be difficult. Because we both know that it triggered a mental breakdown.

Text when you're free, I'll text back I don't plan to do anything today."

It went well than the last time duhh

"I   KNEW   ITTTTT. ASKDBSYDEHJFBUFYGHBJH."

"Bro. YOU DON'T EVEN KNOW"

I did twenty three questions, last time seventeen only

"HOW proud I am rnn

I am so happy you don't even knowww

I'm sorry I didn't ask.

I was travelling BRO."

But at the same time thinking that I might have to do it for one more year could be difficult. Because we both know that it triggered a mental breakdown.

"NAAH, you might not need that, YOU WILL MAKE IT THIS TIME!!"

As is evident from these text messages, everything seemed like it was going to be fine, but I hadn't anticipated that it would take even half the amount of time that it took to make things right.

Well, that's okay, healing takes time," Sharon interrupts me.

"Nah, not just healing, but getting into the process of healing in the first place. But that's for a different day," I tell her.

Journal entry. The therapist session number one. 2023.

Of course she wouldn't let me go on my own. I asked her to wait for me outside because I knew I was going to spill everything that had happened after I failed the test last year, and what came after it, but five minutes into therapy session, somebody knocked at the door and it was nobody other than my mom. The session started by me greeting the therapist and then it was very awkward immediately after that, a year of not socializing does that to you. He asked me what was the problem and why was I there, but before that he asked, "What's your name, and what do you do, like what are you studying right now?"

I told him my name and to the latter I referred to as 'complicated' because it was complicated, but he pushed it so I told him that I am writing a book, and then he asked, "What brings you here?"

"I think I have ADHD," I told him without any hesitation, and he was fascinated with the way I had told him ever so calmly. He then started the assessment and he asked me a lots of questions, and the whole time his face expressions were unreadable. I answered all the questions one after the other and took my time to think on each one of them if needed to.

"Do you feel like you can never wait in a line?"

"I'm not very impulsive in that regard, but that doesn't mean that I don't want to be, let's say for example, I'm filling a bottle of water, I might not say it but I hate waiting till it's filled to the brim. Very often I fill it just halfway, and the whole time I hide my impulsiveness, it comes out as frustration, I am sure to snap at you if you even talk to me normally. I am either late, or very early because I know I can't wait when I'm ready to go so the first option that I have is to get ready early and reach way before time, or delay getting ready and I end up reaching late," I told him.

"Do you sometimes feel like you are zoning out?"

"All the time. Last year my teachers would call me out for it, and I'd have to deny it saying I was just not looking into their direction, while in actuality I had had stopped listening to them a long time ago," I answered.

"Okay now that we're talking about classes and academia, tell me how frequently you answer the questions in class when you know the solution because you can't hold?" he asked.

"Very frequently, although that hasn't happened this year because I didn't knew what to answer for the most part so I kept shut which only heightened some sort of inner frustration, but any other year, very frequently. In high school, it even got to the point that my teachers would actively point in my direction to indicate that I should shut up, and let the person who was about to be asked the question, answer it," I told him, "Why do you ask?"

"Okay tell me about your academic profile, how have you scored for the most part in your life?" he asked.

"For the most part, my average score has been around ninety seven percent, but this past year it wasn't how I wanted it to be, and that's what made me think I might have ADHD," I told him and I went on to tell him about every way I had come to discover that I might have ADHD, and then I asked, "But every article that I read was saying that if you were a great student, you might not have adhd, why is that?"

"That's just an oversimplification. We assess a child's symptoms based on the how well they are able to concentrate, how quickly their minds drift, and how impulsive they are, but academia is not necessarily the only way to do so, we just think it's easier because children spent most of their time in school where all the facets of the disorder are put to test, but sometimes you may even get diagnosed very late in your life. This can happen when you spent most of your life walking on glass beads and egg shells, constantly evaluating everything that you're doing, that keeps ADHD in check, but after a certain point, the real life stuff starts to hit, and being extra aware of everything just isn't enough," he told me.

"And, Ahmad, I'm sorry but I have to tell you that most people don't always have as many thoughts as people with adhd constantly have, and I'm sorry that you found out so late about it, and never had anyone telling you there was such a thing, especially your school. At least your school should have informed your parents because your signs have been somewhat clear; your impulsivity in class, zoning out, and openly critiquing some subjects that you found boring, from what you told me," he said.

"I also need to tell you that, ADHD is often companied by other disorders as well," he said with pity in his eyes, he then started asking a series of questions, and asked my mom some of them, and after I told him that everything just starts to get worse in the winter time, actively omitting the fact that I felt depressed as hell last summer, he came to the conclusion that I might have SAD-seasonal affective disorder.

Before leaving he said that in order to be sure that it is ADHD he might need some scans of my brain to say for sure.

Journal entry the day two of therapy.

I got diagnosed with ADHD today, I don't know why, but I'm happy in an odd way. Today I have landed on the biggest resonating irony of my life ever- ADHD. I show almost all the symptoms of ADHD, all the running away from what I didn't want to study, all the overthinking. I posted on my Instagram today. I watched a couple of videos online to know more about it. I'm so relieved that after knowing that I have it uI no longer have the guilt why was I not being able to get stuff done- although that might be depression, but my therapist didn't say that I have depression, so whatever- I no longer have this constant feeling of guilt with me anymore that I'm being Just Lazy. This is so similar to 2020, I have a condition but back then I didn't think of mental health as openly as I do now, thanks to Selena. Back then I thought that I'd be rejected by the society, my friends and family, but even still I rose from the ashes, and I'm going to do it again, I need to do it for Nostalgia. I no longer carry this feeling of being an alien and a misfit. I still have a long way in all the aspects of my life, not just studies, it's a way of life, my companion now.

Chapter thirteen

Journal entry 21ˢᵗ January, 2023.

You know what I actually made a decision last night that I'll give myself 9 days. And I'll try not to think about Jee and see how I feel without thinking about it. There's more to it but starting with today.

When I woke up today, I got immediately reminded that we are not waking up for jee and that I've given myself these days, I grabbed the bottle of water and poured myself some water. There was a slight concern going through my brain but I subsided it when I sprang like a cork from inside the covers and jumped off the bed. I had my breakfast. I felt kind of sleepy. Because the light went off and the blinds were on and I felt so extremely sleepy. I did. So SAD IS REAL. At this point it's like I need to get the medication for it. I can't settle for therapy or shit. I will make him give me medicine because like you know it's not just because of Jee. I have got real things in the real world to do. Within next ten years I'll most probably be a dad, a husband and all of that shit calls for effective methods so doesn't matter if Jee is over or not, I need help... Back to SAD. LEMME CHECK THE screen time HISTORY. You know I didn't have any direction for today so I started with completing the thriller I started the day before yesterday. Before lunch I was done. I slept in the afternoon. Took a nap intended for 25 minutes but turned into 40 minutes because I couldn't help. I was feeling sleepy. SAD. Thanks to SAD. When I woke up, I wasn't guilty though. You know I wasn't feeling bad and shit. Let's see our YouTube time today. Wow it's only 22 minutes (lol) I wasn't feeling bored to go there and didn't need a refuge.

Journal entry A

Is it that I don't want to do it or that I don't have motivation? No. It's not either of these things.

But the situation is kind of same. Jee or writing a book, I just can't seem to just start it. There are always reasons as to why I don't do it. But at the end I don't.

But reasons for not writing are way less crazy than Jee. For that, the reasons are excruciatingly painful.

I've had my valid reasons for not being able to write to my full potential.

First, I'm stuck between 4 different chapters with entirely different narratives so it's difficult but at the same time, I overthink, ADHD, and I want to use it to my benefit so I actually don't just overthink, I start writing what I think. And these days I think of Romance, how it would feel to have love in life.

While I still write, be creative, I don't feel like I get any work done. Because there are things that are more important while others just aren't.

Second, I've had my engagements.

My cousin came. I don't blame him. I don't cast him as a reason, but I ended up having totally great time with him. He is very sweet. I totally love him. I'm so grateful that I have had a time in my life that I've spent with him, and cared for him. As they say, people who you truly love and care for always stay loyal to you, and he is. He came in calling my name.

But I should have had prioritised right? Yeah I should've. That's something I'm bad at. Totally. I'm so bad at prioritising and choosing between multiple things. I'm bad at making a decision, let alone instant one.

Journal entry B

I've built this relationship with my studies and wellbeing, not a healthy one that is I will determine the amount of happiness I deserve, yeah DESERVE depends on how much I study. I have LITERALLY made myself like that.

Now it doesn't end just there. When I'd get anxiety, I'd link it to my studies in any way and if I studied well, I'd make myself think that there's nothing to be anxious about, and when slightest bit of things would go wrong and I happened to get anxiety the same day, I'd immediately link it to each other. So I had developed some sort of survival mechanism that I should study PERFECTLY in order to not feel down.

YEAH PERFECTLY. I can't believe I did that even after two years of not believing in 'perfect.'

And I did. I tried to. I tried to study as hard as I could after that 11th breakdown because that's what I thought at that time, this is what

I concluded from that time that my depression had everything to do with my studying or not studying, which might as well be true but I also started to believe that if somehow I just study perfectly I could avoid it. But turns out things really aren't PERFECT always like we saw last year, 2022.

I strived for perfection while I forgot about the process. I tried not to be the BEST VERSION OF MYSELF I tried to be the PERFECT PERSON. I knew there were reasons why I hate the idea of perfectionism.

So when I didn't study great, it manifested in the form of uncured anxiety which I'd like to name denial. And it has its own consequences. So basically what I'm trying to say is that, over years I've made studies a deciding factor of my happiness.

Now that if I get anxious sometimes, I feel down, or I get a panic attack, I don't have my coping mechanism with me to make me feel good about it because from 2022, I've not been able to study PERFECTLY (for established reasons), or at all in 2023, so now that I don't study, whenever I am experiencing any of those episodes, I don't have anything to pull me out from it, or link it with. I don't have anything which would make me feel less terrible. I have relied on studies for doing that for so long that now when it is manifesting in its raw form, and not because of just studying or not studying, I don't know a way to find a way out. A whole day passes by and I can't seem to help it.

I definitely need some ways out of it. I have. Tell me a thing, and I know everything about it. Meditation. Stretching. Take a card from the self-love bowl. Reading. Writing. Having Netflix binge. Admiring people over internet. But the problem is I can't think of any of that at that moment maybe because of ADHD, and equally because my main coping mechanism used to be anything related to studies.

Journal entry C

If I'm watching something, I can't just stop.

If I'm reading, I can't just stop.

I have to complete it. And when talking about book, a normal very new reader can't read a book in just one sitting. Or at least that's how it is to me. Because of which two days get doomed.

I can bear not following the schedule by not even starting reading or watching something online than stopping halfway through. I kind of live on extremes..

I sometimes think that I should not do all reading, watching and other stuff at the same time rather I should do one thing at a time but then it gets boring and monotonous. It makes me get carried away and then I don't really appreciate the content or so I think because when you read at breaks, you get to think about what you read.

I listened to hip hop in a rabbit hole. Yeah that's me

I bought a book. Alright. I actually picked up a book called reminders of him. I then picked up another book called some seven husband's and stuff. But then I realised that maybe I expanded my budget and nevertheless I have the e-version of the reminders one. All cool I dropped it and picked the husband one.. But then I saw the book atomic habits. I wanted to buy it. I didn't. I knew why I wanted to buy it. Because it's the very popular self-help book ykk. Andddd I have the e-version of it but it just doesn't feel right to read the e-version of a self-help book. One's got to treat them like textbooks. Umm... alright this is what I did. I searched my e-book collection and couldn't find this husband book. So I bought it. But I still wanted to buy the atomic habits book. I was staring at it. I might as well have had bought it but then I felt awkward asking one more time YK..idk what that is it's like IDC like IDC what I got now but I'm not going to ask him to change it. It happens most of the times. And when I'm where there's less disturbances and less overwhelming crowds and stuff or the people I know, I'll just say it finally but when it comes to the situation like these, like yesterday or with people like the angry or rude ones, I kind of just get paralysed. It's like I get in the survival mode when I have to interact with that sort of shopkeepers.

Now that when I searched it I can actually get this husband book online so I should have bought the atomic one. I tried my best to take a right decision but as you can tell from all of this there was a lot going on inside my brain..

The days since February started have been shit-ful like completely..

And for the most part I've been journaling.

I also spent unnecessary amount of time on Instagram.

I spent time doing ykk like my parents were out so I had to kind of be home alone.

I visited a shrink, actually a therapist.

I did no work.

I watched like 3 movies.

I went to shopping.

I played COC. Actually it wasn't that bad or it was. Idkkk.

I enter my room to follow my schedule but as soon as I set foot inside- it's a bit darker than the other rooms. And I get bored and I hate it. I have SAD.

Journal entry D

Alright let's talk scheduling..

I have this thing that I don't know how much time which task will take and if I attempt to calculate then I'm going to end up in a loop.

Sometimes I will want to do so much and it'll be overwhelming by the end of the day when even half isn't achieved.

Other times it will be so less that I'd feel bad. And then I'd waste energy and resources.

I've been trying to do this scheduling thing but they just never seem to work for me. Gawd this is horrible.

If only this bloody winter could go away.

I just finished watching Titanic and it's the most intense thing I've ever seen in my whole fucking life. So gut wrenching. A classic ROMANTIC TALE, AND OF BRAVERY. I feel so bad for JACK and everybody.

I was gasping the whole time, shockingly.

Journal entry E

I was thinking of how books benefit regardless of the genre, I read every book now with an entirely different perspective. This book I'm reading, it has so many notes in it about life in general. The characters in the books are so relatable, they mess up, they deny, they don't accept at first but then they do but that's not what they truly want so they give themselves time and then finally accept it, just like any normal person, I no longer abide by the definition of 'normal' so I mean these characters are like any average human being, who mess up, and are not perfect.

I was thinking that college might open soon than I thought they would, but idk I get this boiling anxiety from my inside when I think about it. Idk idk.

It's been a month since I officially announced to myself that I'm not doing JEE. To be honest, it has been liberating. So much. I have not taken a moment to appreciate how free I've felt since then. It has not been easy, nothing has been, but at least I don't feel like shit. I waste time and I feel bad that I did because I could have written, it's no longer I could've done something, but something that I hated.

Journal entry F

I think that Being not afraid of life might end up solving half of all of my issues, the personality disorders I might have, introversion, social anxiety; expand my comfort zone. Bad things don't happen just to me, they happen to everybody, all the time. It's a belief that my surroundings especially my family put inside of my head, whenever something bad used to happen they'd be like, "it's always you," *"Kisi aur k saath aisa nhi hota,"* but it's just you. Be it I trip over something, I fall sick, even when I had hair fall, it's me from the birth, like it's my birth fault. BUT bad things happen to everybody. I mean I have heard this before and known this before but adding my own background story to it makes it so different, bad things literally happen to everybody but that doesn't mean you should be afraid of life, bad things are bad things, moments, memories, episodes, it's not whole of the life. Bad things happen to everybody but it depends on who stands back again. Does that mean you don't mourn? No. It doesn't mean that. You should and you have to mourn in order to be fully in control of your emotions. We're being taught this thing that being stoic and non-transparent means you're being strong, and being strong means you're superior, but does it? If you don't show any emotions, what does that mean, aren't you cold hearted, doesn't that person who's dead mean anything to you, or the thing you lost, was it shit's worth? I've invested years and years in trying to be this stoic and almost non transparent figure in order to be what people refer to as "Strong" but it has only brought wreck to me, I've tried to be something I'm totally not, I'm more sensitive and emotional than most of the guys and it has only fucked up my brain to try and have no EMOTIONS at all. If someone fails, not just academically or actually, maybe their judgement fails, what is the one thing people around should do? Here's my case: "I told you so." "Why were you flying so high then?" Was I flying high? Enough is enough! No I wasn't flying high. I can't let society or people in general force me into thinking that I was wrong. I wasn't flying high, I didn't want to talk about it. I didn't feel comfortable in doing so.

Journal entry G

I entered my room, saw that it was a mess and it was overwhelming, folded some clothes, and remembered I have more clothes to pick, came back, put them in the closet. And then found out the zipper was broken, fixed that. And a lot other work while I just wanted to watch TITANIC. !!!

And then I forgot that I had kept my jacket and other stuff in other room and I forgot about them. .

The thing is If I see some task, I know I'm going to forget which I inevitably do, so I try to do it right there and then, and when I can't I get impulsive. It's like how I picked up a trouser to fold that was still wet because I knew I'd forget. I now totally accept it that normal people work normally, and don't have these hassles and that I'm not normal. I need to stop and act like one. Because these struggles have been with me forever and I never thought they were struggles because

I'm so good at hiding things. I need to stop masking so that I address the real problem.

Journal entry H

8.08 am

I feel like shit. I know exactly why.

I was thinking that I have tried to be strong always and bottle up and suck it up. I have always done that and I've always felt like shit when things would go wrong but I've done enough sucking it up and acting strong, it only brought me untreated depression and anxiety.

Now I can't do that. I'm done doing that.

I woke up today and started to feel like shit and I immediately knew why.

I was thinking of all the ways of it towards bad things but I CAN CHOOSE TO BE HAPPY.

And I'm being happy.

"But what changed Ahmad, what happened after the attempt? How was your result?" Sharon asks after reading all the journal entries.

I got my exams back after few days of the test. At first I was hesitant to check the results but the faith that I had developed lately- which was just delusional- that I might make it made me check it and surprisingly what I found was that my score was more than what it was the last time. I had scored a 90 percentile, I had "passed the test" which was just absurd because never in a million years I'd get a seat in any reputed college but who was I kidding, deep down I'd known it, I'd known it all along that it just wasn't meant for me. I took my failure quite well, I handled it well but over time it turned into just denial.

"What changed, what after that?"

"Alisha came in to my life, and a lot of other things happened."

"Is it okay if I ask what?"

"A lot, maybe I'll write a book about it. But what I can say confidently is that sometimes

you have to do things that you never planned to do in the first place so that you ultimately end up doing things that you are meant to be, just like its told in the alchemist, for me it was going through the process of Jee, and what came after it in 2022, but I ultimately landed with the things that I could have never imagined in a million years in my life, which ultimately made the failure a faux-failure"

Epilogue

Year 2036.

I'm checking off the list of the things that I have to do when I go out so that I don't forget anything as I hear a scream from across the hallway coming from Amir's room asking for his favourite pair of jeans while Khushboo is already done with her breakfast and tells her mama, "Geez. Why is this house in shambles today?"

I tousle her hair and sit down where Alizah was sitting before Amir screamed. I ask Khushboo about the things she wants to do as I show her the pictures of Disneyland Park.

"Ahmad, did you clean the dishes?" I hear Alizah scream across the hallway from our bedroom and I holler, "No. And, you haven't eaten anything since yesterday afternoon."

"Buttercup, I'll go see your mama. She's losing it today," I pat Khushi on her head and she responds as she throws her arms in the air and says, "Why is everything chaotic in this house today?" And I cannot help but give her a kiss on the cheek because every time she opens that mouth of hers, something ten times mature than her age comes out.

As I reach near my bedroom, Alizah emerges from the door hysterically and bumps her head on my chest.

"I'm sorry, honey," that's all I can muster.

"Can you please see Amir, baby? I don't even know where the hell my mascara is." She scoffs.

I knock on the door just before entering Amir's room and all I can see is clothes everywhere like a debris of rubble on the post construction site and little Amir sitting on the top of the pile. He looks over his shoulder as he hears the door knob turn and the way the tip of his nose crinkles and his cheeks match the color of lipstick Alizah is wearing I can tell he was about to cry, and he comes running towards me. I pick him up and sit on the edge of Khushi's bed and make him face me.

"What's wrong, lil freind? Let's get you your favourite jeans," I tickle his neck which makes him chuckle which is enough to keep the perspective that I'd take thousand chaotic mornings like today's just to hear this sweet little laugh. I put him in his outfit, "There! You're ready to go, buddy." He kisses my cheek and is nowhere to be seen within the fraction of seconds.

As I'm standing in the room looking around at all the mess that this room, and the household is, I decide to put the clothes in the closet to bring some order as the thought flashes my Brain that fifteen years ago, I'd have been intimidated by this ordeal hadn't I failed and took the decisions that I did that led me here. I take a deep breath and express my gratitude for being able to do this; to do any of this for my family, a family that I would blindly sell myself for, so they could be happy.

This household is in chaos today because Alizah had a late night surgery; when she came back home, she was tired and didn't wake up to the alarm in the morning. Her face was glowing like an amber flame in the sunlight and I couldn't bring myself to wake her up, otherwise by this time, kids are at school, I'm in my office and Alizah's at the clinic.

As I make my way towards the breakfast table where Alizah is feeding Amir, I hear a car honk just outside the front door and I know its Heidi to pick up the kids with her fiancé because kids wanted to go with their favourite aunt and uncle. The plan is to leave at the exact same time. As soon as the kids hear Heidi's voice coming from the car, they become giddy, and Amir attempts to walk away from the breakfast table towards the door but I get hold of him; I pick him up as he cackles and starts to budge while Khushboo makes her way towards the front door. I put Amir down right next to Khushboo and pat them both on their tiny heads, "Go wait in the car, and tell Aunt Heidi to wait just ten more minutes so we can all celebrate your birthday perfectly and together."

Khushboo is four and Amir is three; miraculously both of them were born on the same date but a year apart.

"How do I look, Dida?" Amir Whispers in Khushboo's ear, which I'm sure all of us can hear anyway.

"Khushi turns to him and gives him kiss on the cheek and says, "Handsome as ever, Amir, and Amir returns the gesture by giving her a hug, like the little gentleman he is, and just like that the two of them disappear.

I wipe my hands on a towel as Alizah crosses me after washing her bowl. I grab a hold of her hand and pull her towards me from where we can't be seen and I put my hands on her waist.

"Let me go, Ahmad, we're already very late," she tries to free herself.

"What's the hurry, angry bird?" I say as I put her hands on my shoulders and she looks at me with the light brown eyes that are as beautiful as they were fourteen years ago. We're nine years into our marraige and what this woman has done for me in all these years is impossible to be ever paid back.

I pursue my lips and give her a gentle but passionate kiss and I sense her nerves soothe. I draw back, lift her chin and whisper in her ear, "You need to calm down," and just as the words leave my mouth, both of us laugh.

"Sharon is going to be really proud of you, Ahmad, just like I am," she tells me as we both swing back and forth. "Are we going to stay like this?" She asks.

"I wish we could, just like the old times," I tell her and both of us fell silent. She moves forward, looks me in the eye and says, "Thank you for everything, Ahmad. You've always been the one for me," and I hug her for the precious human she is to me.

"Are you guys done, yet?" Heidi hollers as she stands at the front door.

"Disneyland Park is a thirty-five minutes' drive from here, it's...uh... I think we can make it, before we have to stand in the long line," I say as Alizah and I adjust ourselves in a not so scandalous way.

"Well then, we gotta get moving, folks," Heidi replies and we hit the road.

The end.

ACKNOWLEDGEMENTS

Thanks to everyone who read the book, and are now here reading this. This book was a means of Catharsis and to release pent up frustration. I started writing the UNHINGED project three years ago and over the years my views and opinions have changed drastically, and I take pride in saying that. There were moments when I thought that this book was useless and I was wasting my time with it. This book has been ready for over a year now but perfectionism got the best of me. Countless numbers of time I have gotten back to various sections of this book to edit, add something, or even discard something completely. But I have always known that this was a very important story and I have always felt a inkling to sharing it with the world. What I'm trying to say is that this book might not be a sophisticated piece of literature but the story that I've tried to tell is.

Thank you to me for combating the different battles and finally allowing myself the grace to think that I had to let go of this book so that it becomes OUR book My opinions might still keep on changing even after this book is published but I have grown to be more fearless now.

www.ingramcontent.com/pod-product-compliance
Lightning Source LLC
Chambersburg PA
CBHW061422160726
47995CB00003B/719